TOUGH LESSONS

Hernando Lopez, a teacher at Joseph Soyinka's son's school, is found brutally murdered in his locked classroom with the key in his hand, suspicion rests on Jermaine Letts, an adolescent gang member. With two other sets of keys in circulation, one a master set locked in the school safe and the other in the janitor's possession, how did the assailant get in and out of the school grounds? Joseph decides it's time to get involved and solve the puzzle of who killed Hernando and to find out why.

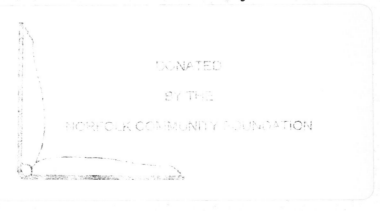

TOUGH LESSONS

by

Chris Freeman

Dales Large Print Books
Long Preston, North Yorkshire,
BD23 4ND, England.

British Library Cataloguing in Publication Data.

Freeman, Chris
    Tough lessons.

    A catalogue record of this book is
    available from the British Library

    ISBN   978-1-84262-768-6

Copyright © Working Partners Two 2009

Cover illustration © Mohamad Itani by arrangement with
Arcangel Images

The moral right of the author has been asserted

Published in Large Print 2010 by arrangement with
Working Partners Two

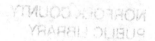

Dales Large Print is an imprint of Library Magna Books Ltd.

Printed and bound in Great Britain by
T.J. (International) Ltd., Cornwall, PL28 8RW

With special thanks to Howard Linskey

For Danielle and Cameron Pope

1

It was Yomi who spotted Eddie first. The big man was down on one knee outside his apartment, hand pressed against the doorframe as if trying to climb to his feet. The retired policeman looked like he had been felled by a low blow. Yomi and his father Joseph wouldn't have seen him at all if they had trusted the lift in the Highbridge Project but no one was foolish enough to use that these days. Instead, they always took the stairs and, from the open landing on the floor below, they could see the old guy, slumped on his knees like a beaten prizefighter.

'What's wrong with Uncle Eddie?' asked Yomi, genuine concern in the boy's voice.

Joseph Soyinka glanced down the corridor at the stooped, silver-haired figure and immediately thought 'heart attack'. His son was already running towards the old man, calling his name and Joseph started after him. He was a tall, athletic black man, who could cover the ground quicker than most men of forty-one. But then, hearing Yomi,

Eddie calmly turned his head and raised his free hand in greeting, and Joseph immediately slowed his run to a walk, relief flooding through him. Eddie grasped the doorframe with his other hand and rocked back and forth until he finally succeeded in hauling himself shakily to his feet.

'I thought you were having a coronary,' said Joseph as he drew nearer. He wanted to chastise the old man, but it was hardly Eddie's fault that Joseph worried too much over him.

'Me?' answered Eddie incredulously. 'Are you kidding?' The silver-haired man wasn't looking at Joseph. He was already engrossed in a mock boxing match with Yomi. 'I just got that stiffness in my joints is all.' He held up a hand to block the excitable blows of the twelve year old with his palm. 'You're more likely to succumb than me, my friend, with your life, all that stress and pressure, sitting on your ass in that cab all day.'

'Thanks,' said Joseph, as he watched Eddie finally succeed in his aim of knocking Yomi's Yankees cap from his head.

'Hey!' said the boy. 'Don't handle the merchandise, Eddie.' But he was laughing along with his honorary uncle.

'What are you doing out here on your

hands and knees anyhow?' asked Joseph, then he stopped abruptly because the reason suddenly became all to clear. 'Oh,' he said, as he surveyed the once-pristine door of his friend's apartment. The white door had been defaced by graffiti, a huge, lurid symbol daubed on it in red paint. Joseph could clearly make out the letters CK with a downward arrow at the end.

Though the symbol meant nothing to him, it had an ominous, threatening look. Some of the paint had run and the surplus had rolled down the length of the door in little streams that looked like streaks of blood. 'What the hell is...?'

'Kids,' said Eddie, too quickly. 'Ain't nothing.'

'Looks like something to me,' said Joseph, as he surveyed the handiwork uneasily. 'Is this a gang tag?'

Eddie just shrugged, as if it was of no consequence to him who had defaced his door but the concern in his eyes told a different story. 'Just some punk with a spray can who can't pass a door without messing it up...' He opened his palms as if that was sufficient explanation for the huge, red symbol on his front door.

Strange how they passed everybody else's

on your floor, but yours was the only door with graffiti, thought Joseph. Why would they target Eddie? Not many in their South Bronx project knew Eddie Filan used to be a cop back in New Jersey, but maybe the gangs had discovered the truth. It seemed that almost forty years enforcing the law on the other side of the Hudson could have earned Eddie a little unwanted attention from the gangs. Joseph doubted it though. There was more to this, he was sure of it, but he let it slide as that's the way Eddie wanted it.

Joseph's friend affected disinterest. He nodded at the brush and the pot of white paint at his feet. 'I'll have it gone in no time. I was going to paint the door anyhow so it makes no difference to me.'

'Still...'

'It ain't nothing, Joseph, quit worrying.' There was a mild rebuke in the words and Joseph decided it might be time to drop the subject. 'Anyhow, where you guys going on this cold morning?'

'School,' answered Yomi, and he pulled a face.

'Ah yes, remind me to light a candle for the poor teachers of Antoinette Irving Junior High.'

'Why?' asked the boy.

'Because they have to force an education into the thick skulls of no-mark, little kids who wanna be any place but there, that's why,' and he grabbed Yomi, wrapping a pasty arm round his neck, and pretended to bang his fist into the laughing youngster's head to illustrate his point.

'Come on, Yomi, we're going to be late,' Joseph called out, then he asked Eddie, 'You want to call in for dinner tonight? There'll be more than enough for three.'

'Oh, I don't want to be no trouble,' said Eddie.

It was always the same, thought Joseph. Two or three times a week they went through this elaborate ritual. Eddie wanted to come to dinner and they wanted to have him there, but it was always a struggle to get him to agree.

'We'd be glad to have you,' Joseph assured him, and before Eddie could bring up the subject of paying his way, he added, 'We'll provide the food, you bring the whisky. That okay?'

Apparently it was. Eddie seemed happy with this arrangement. He had been happier still to complete the education of his friend from Lagos when he first introduced him to the unequalled joys of Irish whisky. 'Never

Scotch Joseph,' he would caution. 'That's inferior witches' brew made by heathens in skirts. You're lucky I met you in time to give you that piece of sage advice before you strayed from the path of righteousness and were lost for ever.'

For Joseph, the numbing effect of a large glass of whisky at the end of a long day was often what he needed. On some nights he couldn't sleep at all, others saw his rest disturbed by nightmares from the old country. The whisky dulled the pain and helped to keep the memories of his dead wife at bay. He knew Apara would have understood that.

Joseph stole one last glance at the tag on his friend's door. The sight disturbed him, for it could surely mean only one thing. One of the many gangs that were slowly taking over the Highbridge Project had singled Eddie out, putting their very own mark of Cain on his door and no one else's. What would happen to the old man next – a bit of petty vandalism, a break-in, or worse? Joseph made a conscious decision to put those thoughts from his mind, as he coaxed his son along the corridor and down the next flight of stairs.

From the moment they arrived at Antoinette Irving, it was clear this wasn't going to be a normal school day. The four police cars, parked at odd angles in front of the school, were testimony to that. One thing was certain; they weren't here to investigate the junior high school's truancy record.

The squad cars had been abandoned right outside the front door, their lights flashing madly. One officer stood guard over them while the others were occupied by whatever was going on inside the main building. He was the unlucky one, forced to stamp his feet and clasp his gloved hands together like he was applauding something, as he tried to stave off the cold from the New York winter's most unforgiving day so far. Around the cars, a gaggle of parents stood talking animatedly amongst themselves. Some clutched their kids, as if the danger might still be present, but Joseph could tell from the demeanour of the officer standing outside the old fifties-built, grey stone building that this was no Columbine-style siege, with mad gun men still on the loose. This was a crime scene.

Something very serious had to have happened inside the school. The way the cops had sent four cars instead of one, the level of urgency displayed by leaving them so hastily, in a seemingly random manner, meant something major was going on inside

Antoinette Irving. He doubted very much if any of its eight hundred students would be entering the school building today.

As Joseph eased his cab into a quiet corner of the car park, he told Yomi to stay close. The wide-eyed boy nodded, though his gaze stayed on the two grim-faced police officers who walked out of the school to confer with their colleague. They were all dressed in the same standard-issue, quilted jackets in an effort to keep out the chill. Yomi seemed more interested in the standard-issue side arms that hung from their belts. All of them carried the Smith & Wesson 5906 semi-automatics that cops in New York had favoured for years now. Eddie was a big fan of the 9mm semi-automatic, pouring scorn on the new breed of policemen who preferred lighter, showier models like the Sig Sauer and the Glock. There was a brief discussion while the officers reached agreement, then they fanned out in an attempt to push the concerned parents and their bewildered children back to form a wider perimeter outside the ancient school.

As Joseph and his son drew closer, they passed a pretty little girl from Yomi's class. Laura Williams was a sixth grader like his son. Her long, honey-coloured hair was half hidden by a woollen bobble hat, there were tears streaked down her face and both of her arms were wrapped tightly round her bright-red school bag, as she clutched it to herself. It looked like she was worried someone might steal the bag, but Joseph knew that wasn't it. He had seen people in shock before and Laura Williams was hugging her bag for comfort. Her father, Merve, stood dumbly by her side, a hand on her shoulder, as if he had no idea how to console his little girl. He looked pale, perhaps even in shock himself. But what had he heard? Then Joseph spotted Emilio Romero, another father who lived on their project. He walked by with his young son, having evidently decided there was no point in hanging around.

'Somebody sliced up a teacher,' he told Joseph indelicately, making no attempt to lower his voice, despite the presence of their children. Romero sounded almost gleeful, like he couldn't wait to be the one to impart the grim news to others.

Joseph's thoughts instantly turned to his son's teacher Brigitte but, before he could ask Romero which teacher had been sliced up, the man was gone. Please, he thought, don't let it be her and the old, all-too-familiar feeling of dread settled over him.

He scanned the building anxiously, his eyes settling on the room Brigitte De Moyne used to mark homework at the end of every school day, a room he had been in recently. There were three large glass windows here that overlooked the car park. Joseph noticed the one at the far end had been defaced, but this wasn't graffiti and there were no gang tags here. He peered intently at the long, red, vertical mark that was smeared down the inside of the window. Even from this distance it couldn't be anything but blood.

2

'Stay with me,' said Joseph firmly and he steered his son towards the rear of the school. Though he far from relished the prospect of bringing a twelve year old onto a crime scene, Joseph was damned if he was going to wait outside with no news of Brigitte De Moyne while his anxiety continued to grow. Since he couldn't be sure whether the attacker was still around, he wasn't letting his son out of his sight, leaving Yomi standing in front of the school in the South Bronx on his own. Joseph skirted along the side of the building, around the corner that looked out onto the playing fields. The grass on the football pitches, between the school's two main buildings, had been frosted white and the water in its pond frozen hard over night. You could probably walk across it in safety now if you chose to. Joseph led Yomi to a side door that opened out onto the sports fields. There was no police presence here and the door was unlocked so Joseph quickly opened it and they went inside.

Father and son walked down a wide, empty corridor with a heavily waxed floor that was lined on either side with metal lockers. Dominating one wall was a glass display case that held sporting trophies from a more illustrious era. The Junior High took its kids from the surrounding area and, to the eternal shame of its principal, the fifth to eighth graders of this neighbourhood seemed to view sport as something inflicted on them rather than a noble pursuit to be strived at for its own sake. There were no famous sportsmen and women among its notable alumni, only a soap star, a newsreader, and a convicted serial killer, the latter being easily the most talked about.

Joseph knew his way around the building

from the parents' evenings he'd been encouraged to attend, although at Antoinette Irving they always seemed pretty stunned when anyone showed up. He was heading for the office Brigitte used for marking homework. Joseph had slowly come to know the teacher well and they had struck up a friendship as Yomi progressed through the school.

Joseph rounded the corner, his son a yard or two behind him, struggling to keep up with his father's stride. They were immediately confronted by a small group of police and shocked school staff who were standing around looking helpless. They were in a large, open area that had the main door of the school building on one side and a row of classrooms on the other. Joseph's gaze shot past them to one of the schoolrooms. It had two glass panels in the door, separated by a horizontal wooden strut and, like the window he'd seen earlier, they were both smeared with blood. It looked like someone bleeding heavily had fallen against them. Joseph's gaze went to the floor outside the classroom. There were distinct drops of blood on the tiny, wooden tiles and larger splashes on the pale-cream walls. It appeared that somebody had been stabbed in the corridor and had desperately tried to reach the sanctuary of the classroom? Instinctively, Joseph used an arm to prevent Yomi from getting too close, but his son could not have failed to see the telltale signs of the attack.

'How'd you get in here?' Principal Decker demanded, as if Joseph's presence in the school building was a personal affront to him. Decker was a tall, thin, serious man who wore wire-framed glasses over his long nose and sported a permanent frown, in case you'd forgotten how much responsibility rested on his bony shoulders. He considered Antoinette Irving to be his own personal fiefdom and, though he knew Joseph as one of the few parents to attend the extra curricular activities he was always so anxious to promote, he now evidently viewed him as little more than a trespasser.

'Who's he?' demanded a gaunt police officer before Joseph could answer the principal's question. It was asked as if Joseph wasn't standing right there in front of them both.

'One of our parents,' answered Decker, making the last word sound like an irritant. Decker always managed to convey the feeling that he could run the school exactly as he wanted, if it wasn't for the intrusion of meddling parents and their inconvenient children, who insisted on turning up there each morning to ruin the well-ordered structure of his day.

The cop advanced on Joseph and said, 'Arms in the air.'

Joseph complied, and the cop patted him down for weapons. He seemed satisfied when he didn't find any. Thankfully he didn't bother to pat down Yomi, who seemed quite alarmed at the prospect, but who wouldn't be scared of cops at his age?

'It don't matter.' The cop was speaking to Decker. 'We gonna need to speak to everybody.' Then he addressed Joseph directly once more. 'Just stand back and don't touch nothing, you hear.'

Joseph ignored this. 'What happened?'

'Teacher been stabbed,' said the cop routinely, like he'd been telling people all morning.

'Serious?' But Joseph knew the answer already.

'Dead,' said the cop.

Joseph wanted to ask who was dead but his mouth had gone dry. Surely it couldn't be happening again.

'Joseph?' the voice was soft, female, puzzled and coming from the side of the room.

Joseph turned to see Brigitte De Moyne

standing there in front of him, completely unharmed. Relief flooded through him.

'Brigitte, I thought...' and he didn't need to finish the sentence for she understood immediately.

'I use the adjoining room,' she said, and he realised in his concern that he had been mistaken. Hers was the next window along. He put his arm round his son's shoulders and coaxed Yomi towards Brigitte, putting a little distance between them and the flustered Principal, steering his son away from the blood on the walls in the process.

At school, Brigitte De Moyne tied up her long hair, wore little make-up and sported the practical, sexless clothes she favoured for teaching but she was still an undeniably attractive woman. A brunette in her mid thirties who was able to turn heads even now, judging by the way the cop was looking at her.

'Who then?' asked Joseph.

'Hernando Lopez.' She said it sadly, and Joseph got an instant image of the diminutive maths teacher, a popular and gentle soul who nonetheless seemed eminently capable of controlling the tougher kids he came up against on a day-to-day basis.

'That's terrible. What happened?'

'They are saying someone got into the building after everyone else had gone home and stabbed Hernando. I can't believe it, Joseph; he was such a nice, sweet, gentle guy. They found his body this morning. He'd locked himself in the room...' Perhaps she was too upset to put it into words or maybe it was the presence of Yomi that prevented her from finishing, but the implication was clear. Someone had knifed the teacher in the corridor. He had managed to escape to his classroom but only succeeded in delaying the inevitable. Hernando had bled to death in his own classroom.

'Are you all right, son?' Joseph asked Yomi. His boy looked shocked and his eyes kept returning to the marks on the wall. Now that he knew Brigitte was safe, Joseph regretted bringing his son onto the crime scene but there was nothing that could be done about that now. 'Son?'

Yomi finally heard him, but he was too stunned to speak. He simply nodded quickly. Joseph turned back to Brigitte.

'Who would want to do something like this?'

'Police seem to think it was one of the kids.' She shook her head in wonder at the world. 'I heard he had a row with one of the older ones recently. He took a knife from a boy in class, I don't know who, but you wouldn't think that would be reason enough to...' Again it was difficult to find the words. 'I don't know if it was the same knife that...'

'You tell this to the cops?' Joseph interrupted, so she didn't have to finish the sentence.

'Of course.'

Just then, the slight figure of Ardo Piloyan wandered almost apologetically into view. The Janitor looked a little lost, glancing about him bemusedly, as if he did not know what to do with all these people in his way. Ardo's grey overalls were always too big for him and his cheap shoes squeaked on the floor he himself had waxed until it shone like a mirror. The little Armenian knew Joseph well, for he had a room a couple of floors above him in the same project. His lined face broke into a grim little smile of recognition and he walked over to the first friendly face he saw. 'Terrible, terrible thing,' he said in heavily accented English. 'Damn gangs respect nothing in this city.'

'They know for sure it was one of the kids?' asked Joseph.

'That's what the cops are talking about,' confirmed Ardo. 'A man like Mr Lopez, who else gonna be his enemy? I tell them it is the gangs, they are everywhere and they tell me it's a problem all over the city. They say it's how they settle things when two members of the same gang got a dispute, with knives. That tall cop, he tells me it looks like one of them had a dispute with his poor teacher.' Ardo shook his head. 'They leave their sign all over the place. Know how many times I got to wash tags off or paint over them?' he asked rhetorically. So Eddie's door was not the only place where gang tags were appearing.

'What do they look like, these gang tags?'

'They scratch letters into my woodwork with knives or spray them on with canned paint. It's just letters and numbers, mostly.'

'What letters?'

'DDP, LK, CK,' he counted them off on his fingers until he tired of it. 'Who knows what they're saying. They don't mean shit to me.' Then he remembered Brigitte was standing there and demurred apologetically. 'Excuse me.'

Joseph had been listening to Ardo, but all the while he had been carefully scanning the room. It was as Ardo was concluding his explanation of the gang graffiti that Joseph saw it. There, high above the blood-smeared doorframe, sprayed onto the concrete wall in red paint was a miniature version of the tag on Eddie's door. The red letters CK up so high that Joseph wondered how they could have reached there without being caught in the act. He hadn't spotted it at first, despite its jarring presence on the white wall, because his eye had naturally gone to the blood on the floor and the door instead. The same gang that sprayed their tag on Eddie's door was active in the school and Antoinette Irving had just had its first murder. Coincidence? Joseph hoped so, for Eddie's sake.

But it looked like the cops were already following the line that Lopez was stabbed by a kid in a gang, mainly because he took a knife off some boy and had no obvious enemies. They needed to be more cautious than that thought Joseph. He had seen this before, people jumping to instant conclusions right at the beginning of an investigation and sticking with them even when the evidence started to point in another direction. Sometimes it clouded their judgement so bad they could no longer see straight. He was willing to bet that one of the police officers had picked up on Brigitte's statement about the confiscated knife and the row with a pupil then added it to the circumstantial evidence provided by Ardo, of gangs roaming unchecked along the corridors of Antoinette Irving. They had come up with a half-baked theory already, even before Hernando Lopez's blood was dry on the school's walls. The uniformed guys had got it into their head that Lopez was murdered by a gang member. Well, maybe he was, thought Joseph, and maybe he wasn't, but it was surely too early to rule anything out. Telling their half-baked theories to anyone who would listen wasn't going to help them complete their investigation.

The principal called Ardo's name and the janitor shuffled over to be given a task Joseph couldn't make out. Up until now, Yomi had been completely silent while he digested the news of the murder but now he suddenly said, 'I need to go the bathroom.'

'Are you okay?'

Yomi nodded glumly. 'Yeah.'

Poor kid must have been in shock hearing such terrible news about his teacher, thought Joseph. Thanks to his father's misguided concern for Brigitte, Yomi had even seen the blood.

'Okay,' said Joseph and Yomi wandered away, leaving his father alone with Brigitte. Joseph made sure his son was out of earshot then he lowered his voice. 'You want to cancel tonight? I'd understand if you did.'

'Cancel? No,' she said emphatically. 'Absolutely not.' Then she seemed to think for a moment. 'Postpone maybe. I mean I still want to do it.' She paused before asking him unsurely, 'Do you?'

'Yeah,' he said. 'I do,' and she nodded.

'Couple of days?' she asked.

'Couple of days,' he agreed.

Neither of them seemed to be able to add anything to that. Instead they simply stood to one side while they watched the NYPD go about its work of Protecting and Serving the public. Eventually a tall man, clutching a large, leather bag approached one of the uniformed officers. He looked like a doctor and Joseph guessed this must be the pathologist. The cops checked his credentials and eventually he was admitted to the crime scene, ducking under the yellow tape that criss-crossed the door.

Joseph realised Yomi had still not returned from the bathroom and instinctively felt something was not quite right. 'Excuse me,' he said to Brigitte, then he followed the path taken by his son.

'Don't leave the building,' ordered the gaunt cop gruffly and again Joseph did not bother to acknowledge him.

As he reached the boy's toilet, Yomi was just emerging. The boy started when he saw his father. 'What?' he asked a little too guiltily, and Joseph could see the worry in his eyes.

'I got to go, too,' said Joseph. 'Wait over there with Brigitte,' and his son uncharacteristically did as he was told.

Joseph walked into the bathroom and went straight past the row of urinals and wash-basins without stopping until he reached the two cubicles at the far end of the room. Yomi had been gone too long and he looked too furtive for Joseph's liking. On a hunch, Joseph chose the furthest cubicle from the door and walked in. It was an old-fashioned toilet with a box cistern and everything looked normal enough. He was about to leave and check the second cubicle when he noticed the faint imprint on the toilet seat that was just catching the light. There was the dim outline of a child-sized shoe and a spec of fresh mud. Someone had climbed up onto it recently. He glanced up at the old cistern with its flush chain dangling down. The chain was still moving slightly, which meant some-one had brushed against it just a moment ago.

Joseph stood up straight and carefully

lifted the lid of the cistern. Yomi would be just about tall enough to manage the same manoeuvre but, unlike his father, he would not be able to see inside. Joseph peered down, saw something metallic in the water and instantly got a sick feeling deep in the pit of his stomach. Under the surface was a knife and Joseph had a good idea who it belonged to.

3

The sick feeling in his stomach stayed with Joseph as he walked back to the scene outside the classroom for there could surely only be one explanation. Unless he was very much mistaken, his twelve-year-old son, pride of his life, had taken to carrying a knife around with him. He knew he should march over to Yomi right now, take him away from the crime scene and tear into the boy for being such a damned idiot but, just for the moment, he was too shocked to conjure the right words. Detective Joseph Soyinka had seen some grim sites with the Nigerian Police Force on the streets of

Lagos. There'd been bloated corpses fished out of rivers after they had been missing for days, mutilated victims of gangland attacks who were too scared to name those responsible for their terrible injuries, murder victims with gun-shot wounds in their heads the size of eight-balls. All of it he had been able to dispassionately describe to his superior officers in the Nigerian Police Force, but this? How do you find the words to accuse a twelve year old, your own flesh and blood, of carrying a lethal blade and then ditching it at a murder scene to avoid the police finding it? He couldn't do that just yet. Not here, not in front of everybody.

He glanced over at Yomi, who was still standing next to Brigitte De Moyne but looking straight back at his father, searching for a clue to whether Joseph might know what he had been up to. He could see it in the child's eyes but he managed to mask his own emotions, putting on a dispassionate face, even as his mind was reeling. Yomi still looked like a child to his father, as the diminutive female history teacher still towered over him, yet he was already caught up in the worst parts of the culture of the South Bronx. If you were a man here, you carried a knife. How many years before Yomi decided that, if you were a real man, then you had to carry a gun as well? Just then Joseph wanted to take his son by the hand, climb into the cab and drive as far away from New York as possible. And where would that get them? How long would they survive if he had no job, no money, no home? The tiny apartment in the Highbridge Project wasn't much but it was a couple of rooms with a roof and four walls and the heating worked just well enough to keep out the biting cold of winter. Joseph knew he couldn't give up even that small comfort lightly.

Whatever further thoughts he may have had about the knife and his son's stupidity, they were suddenly interrupted by a small commotion at the main door, for someone was making an entrance. Two male detectives, rugged-looking types in leather jackets, burst through the big glass doors with unnecessary haste. Why were they in such a hurry? wondered Joseph. Who were they trying to impress with their self-important bustle? The uniformed officers all straightened, as if god or at the least the President of the United States was about to enter the room after them, but it was a far more familiar figure who eventually breezed in, the tail of her coat trailing behind her.

Assistant Chief McCavity had a look of steely determination on her face, as if she had come to single-handedly save the day and you had better not get in her way while she went about it. She was in her mid forties and her demeanour was that of a woman at the peak of her powers. She squinted at them all, as if the cold wind that had thrown her auburn hair into such an unruly mess was still blowing into her pale, hard face. The wind was probably the only thing in New York that dared defy her these days, thought Joseph, for he'd dealt with this woman before.

'I am Assistant Chief McCavity of the 41st Precinct,' she told the room. 'And, as of right now, I am in charge of this investigation.' She turned to the nearest uniform. 'What have we got here?'

'A teacher ... er ... ma'am.' Nervousness made him confer with his notebook, to ensure he made no error that could be held against him at a later date. 'One Hernando Lopez, fatally stabbed with a knife last night after the school day was over. We think he was marking books and a person or persons unknown attacked him out here in the corridor. Maybe he went to the john or something.' He realised from her unsympathetic glare that she was unimpressed by his hypothesising.

'Who knows?' he said weakly, quick to surrender the actual detective work to her. 'There's blood on the floor and the walls and we found a knife that appears to be the murder weapon. Looks to us like he managed to get into his classroom after he was stabbed and lock the door behind him, but he bled to death in there. His key was still in the lock when the janitor found him this morning.'

When the gaunt officer had finished, everybody glanced over at McCavity like she was a regular Nancy Drew and was about to crack the case in an instant.

'What did he teach?' she asked.

'Maths,' said the officer.

'Mmmm,' she pondered, as if it might somehow be of importance, then she noticed Joseph for the first time and narrowed her eyes. 'Mr Solinka.' Joseph still didn't know if she always got his name wrong deliberately or if it was a genuine error. 'What are you doing here? Not up to any of your amateur sleuthing, I hope. This isn't *Murder She Wrote.*' The two detectives chuckled dutifully at her weak joke, but nobody else did.

'My son is a pupil here,' said Joseph. 'I was bringing him to school.'

'Small world,' she said.

'Excuse me, I'm the principal.' Decker

stepped forwards, hand outstretched, looking perturbed at the connection between them and the fact McCavity had ignored him ever since her arrival. 'Do you know each other?'

'Mr Solinka gave us his assistance with a case once.' McCavity said it like Joseph had jotted down the registration of a getaway car or supplied the description of a burglar. Whereas they both knew he had successfully completed the investigation of a girl's murder and saved McCavity from sending the wrong man to jail for life. Then he had retreated from the scene allowing her to boast on TV about the apprehension of a major drug dealer, whose last drop had been handed to her by Joseph on a plate. He'd known at the time he would not get much credit. In fact he didn't want any. Who could survive on the Highbridge Project if they were a known friend of the NYPD? Look what had happened to Eddie.

'Really?' asked the principal dubiously, as if this somehow made Joseph a criminal himself.

McCavity didn't bother to answer him. Instead, she went into command mode. 'You,' she told the nearest uniform. 'Take me to the body and make sure nobody gets near it without my say-so. And you,' she jabbed her finger at another policeman, who looked up nervously. 'Make sure there's desks and chairs set up in the refectory. We're gonna need to talk to people and take statements. You two.' The remaining uniformed officers were swept up by her gaze. 'Make sure no one outside leaves and bring them all inside before anyone dies from hyperthermia. We don't want any more bodies on our hands.' McCavity was completely oblivious to the feelings of the grieving colleagues of Lopez, who were still standing around her in shock. 'Get everybody into the refectory and take a statement from every teacher and parent. I want details from everybody.'

'Everybody?' asked the officer rashly. 'But that'll take...'

'As long as it will take,' said McCavity coldly. 'Start now, do it,' and he obviously thought it wise not to contradict her further.

The uniformed officers scuttled away and McCavity walked into the murdered teacher's classroom flanked by her two detectives. They looked like bodyguards protecting a queen.

Joseph sighed. He had clearly heard McCavity's order and could hardly claim to have misunderstood it, but right now he couldn't afford to hang around. Besides, he could offer no insight into the murder of Hernando Lopez. The uniformed cop was right. It would take an age to extract statements from everybody and the process was unlikely to uncover much in the way of hard evidence. It had to be done however. Joseph understood this more than anybody. He reasoned that since he had no information on the murder, he would actually be hindering the police if he stuck around, wasting their valuable time. That was how he justified his actions when he went over to Yomi and led him quietly from the building, 'Obviously there's not going to be any school this morning,' he informed his son. 'Freddie's mother is over there. I'm going to ask her if she will take you for a few hours.'

'Why?' asked the boy. 'Where are you going?'

'There's some place I've got to be,' he said firmly.

'Right then, Mr Soyinka. Take this bottle, take your time and return it to me when you have filled it at least halfway,' said the young girl in the white coat matter-of-factly. She smiled sweetly as she handed over the little plastic vial. Joseph was a grown man yet he still found this kind of thing acutely embarrassing. Maybe it was because he was being asked to piss into a tiny plastic bottle by a cute female doctor, who was surely no older than twenty-five that made the situation more uncomfortable. Joseph had reached the age where, like police officers, doctors were starting to look younger, especially the female ones.

'Certainly, miss,' he said, his nervousness making him formal, as it often did.

Joseph went into the men's bathroom, resisted the temptation to whistle as he waited for nature to take its course, then returned the specimen bottle and was told to report to another room.

'They are waiting for you,' the girl said ominously.

Joseph stood in the corridor outside for a moment, straightened his tie and pulled the knot a little tighter. His best white shirt had been ironed into creases you could cut your finger on and he tried hard to ignore its fraying cuffs. Right now, buying a new shirt for an interview was a lower priority than keeping the heating turned on and putting food in their refrigerator.

'Come in, Mr Soyinka, sit down,' instructed the grey-suited young man. He had a hundred-watt smile that he could somehow turn on and off again in an instant. 'I'm Karl from Human Resources, he announced brightly.' Whatever that meant, thought Joseph. Like many men of his generation, he wondered why they just couldn't go on calling it personnel. He resented being referred to as a resource. 'And this is Detective Moreno,' he introduced a bored-looking older colleague sitting next to him. 'A very experienced serving officer in the NYPD. We like to come at these interviews from both angles. I'm sure you understand.'

'I do,' said Joseph, and he did. He would be interviewed by someone who knew the job but would rather be anywhere but there, and somebody who had no idea what the job entailed but still considered himself an expert. Joseph managed to hide his scepticism. He had to. Since his arrival in America his burning ambition had been to join the NYPD, on the lowest rung if that's what it took to become a police officer again. Then he could steadily work his way through up the ranks, using his investigative experience from his homeland to good effect, until he was finally back to his former rank of detective. But it hadn't been easy. His first application had become stalled by bureaucracy and the intervening months had been filled with endless hours at the wheel of a cab.

'I'm pleased to say you performed well in your previous interview and you had some very strong results on both your aptitude and attitudinal tests,' said Karl.

Was Joseph mistaken or was there just the slightest hint of surprise in his interviewer's voice?

'Let's assume that nothing untoward comes back from your pee test shall we,' and he grinned self-consciously, as if he expected both men to laugh at this but they did not. 'Yes,' he said, 'I think we'll take that as a given,' and he nodded reassuringly. 'There are just a few more questions we have to put to you now.'

'Like why you want to be a cop?' asked the detective abruptly.

Joseph thought for a moment, then said, 'I can't remember a time when I didn't want to be a cop. It was just something that was always there from a very early age. I always had this clear view of what a cop was.'

'And what was that?' asked the suit from HR.

'Someone who made a difference. I didn't want to be somebody who got up every morning and went off to work only to kill time in meetings until the end of the day, talking about rivets or paperclips.' In other words someone like you, Karl, he could have added. 'I needed more than that. I wanted a job where I could go home at night, every night, and feel like I made a difference. As soon as I was old enough I applied to join the NPF. I was a police officer in Lagos for twenty years, and I did the job well, if you don't mind me saying so.'

'Still think you made a difference?' asked the veteran cop.

'Yes,' answered Joseph immediately. 'It wasn't always easy, but yes.'

'Every day?' continued the old cop.

'Not every day, no. That only happens on TV, when things are wrapped up nicely at the end of each episode. Real life isn't like that.'

'There is the matter of your age,' said the HR guy. 'We don't normally solicit applications from anyone over thirty-five.'

'Really? I'd have thought you might be more open-minded. There's no substitute for experience in police work. Thirty-five is hardly retirement age after all.' The veteran cop's eyes seemed to twinkle, as if he was stifling a smile. The young HR guy carried on regardless. 'I was going to add that in your case the age limit is of less importance, as your previous experience is highly relevant. Your physical examination revealed you to be in pretty good shape for a man of your age,' he added, as if he were a junior doctor addressing a geriatric patient in his ward.

Joseph surveyed the pasty HR man for a moment and silently counted to ten in his head before replying. Even then he couldn't resist it. 'Police work is pretty active. Sometimes the bad guys run away,' he said, as if he was explaining the hidden nature of the job to his interviewer, who watched him with only the slightest furrowing of the brow. Clearly Karl didn't know for sure if he was being mocked. Moreno meanwhile looked away and smothered a laugh.

Joseph continued. 'I've tried to keep myself in good shape. I run, lift weights...'

Karl was nodding supportively. 'Good,' he said, as if he himself had lifted anything heavier than a pen and clipboard all week.

'In many ways,' said Joseph dryly, 'I consider myself in better shape than a man of twenty-five with a desk job.' There was a moment, just a moment, when Joseph feared he might have gone too far. Karl would surely realise he was being derided by the older man. Moreno was faking a coughing fit to contain his laughter, but Karl missed the connection between them. Joseph managed to stare the desk man down, as if every word had been part of a plain and simple answer to a reasonable question.

The uncomprehending HR man continued. 'We do have one or two other concerns however, chief among them the small matter of references from your previous employment with the Nigerian Police Force.' He spoke the words like he expected to be congratulated for remembering those complex facts about Joseph's previous life.

Joseph's heart sank when the references were mentioned. 'Is there something wrong with my references?'

'The fact that we didn't receive any,' said the experienced, serving detective without disguising his suspicion. There was no trace of a smile now.

'Well I thought that had been cleared up,' said Joseph, already fearing the worst. 'My former superiors didn't send them off in time for my first application so you turned me down but that was nearly a year ago and I was under the impression it had all been addressed.' It should have been addressed. It had taken Joseph numerous phone calls and a couple of blatant lies, spread over several days, before he had finally been able to get Opara to take his call. When cornered, his former captain had been unduly evasive. This was the same man who had promised him every assistance with his application for a new job in a police force in America, as long as Joseph agreed to leave Lagos immediately before his powerful enemies in high places made the captain's life intolerable. Besides, as he had painstakingly explained to Joseph, he could no longer guarantee the safety of his star Detective, or that of his son. He didn't need to remind Joseph about Apara.

'You made every effort to contact this captain of yours, did you?' asked Karl.

'I spoke to him, yes, and he swore to me he would send you a reference, confirming my faultless service record and years of good conduct.' At least that is what the captain had said on the telephone, as he had squirmed and apologised then blamed it all on the bloated bureaucracy around him. Clearly he never had any intention of actually delivering on this heartfelt promise.

'Mmm, well I'm afraid that reference has not actually been forthcoming,' said the man from HR, his smile had faded to just below forty watts now.

'Why do you think that was?' asked Detective Moreno, evidently forgetting that Joseph was not the suspect in one of his investigations.

'I have no idea,' answered Joseph, for he didn't want to explain to these strangers the true extent of the corruption he had encountered during his career with the NPF. It was like turning over a stone in a beautiful garden only to find something foul wriggling underneath. Joseph, the star detective, had been asked to police the police, watch the detectives and root out the corrupt officers in the Nigerian Police Force. He had been promised it all, total cooperation, resources, funding, access to the great and good, who were all pinning their hopes on him to clean out the cess pit.

'Roam the country, Detective Soyinka. Pluck the rotten apples from the tree,' he had been urged by Captain Opara, 'Bring the big men the results they are looking for, Joseph, end the stench of corruption that has been beneath our noses for too long.'

Unfortunately Joseph proved to be too able an investigator for the big men's liking. They had been hoping for a couple of token arrests; a detective constable on the take in Victoria, a detective sergeant who accepts drug money to turn a blind eye when a drop is going down in Abuja. Instead, he had done his job far too diligently and unearthed a complex web of corruption that went right up through the senior ranks of the NPF, to the politicians and senior officials of the ministries. This they had not bargained for. Joseph's investigation had begun to threaten pension plans and undeclared second incomes delivered to banks in far-flung locations, beyond the prying eyes of the tax collectors. Men in positions of great power began to feel nervous. Joseph wasn't so much removing rotten apples from the branches as threatening to uproot the whole damn tree and bring it crashing to the ground for ever.

Joseph had been forced to accept he would never know who hired the hit man that came looking for him that night. All he was left with in the morning were the charred remains of his timber home and the memories of the poor, dear wife who had been inside the building when they calmly poured gasoline though his door and set it alight. How many times had he gone over it in his mind since? If only he had been there that day instead of chasing down a lead in Abuja, perhaps he could have saved her. If Yomi had not been at his grandmother's that night he would have lost him too. He would have been robbed of everything; home, wife and son in one terrible night but Yomi had been spared. Joseph had learned to wrap his whole life around that small mercy.

Any chance Joseph might have had of finding the man who gave the order died, along with the hit man, who was himself cut down in a hail of bullets, seconds after his brand-new Mercedes was run off the road by a person or persons unknown. Oba Matusa's bullet-riddled corpse had barely turned cold before Captain Opara was summoning his department's untouchable detective to offer him a simple choice, exile from his home for ever or the strong likelihood that his body would be the next one on the slab in the mortuary.

How could Joseph explain that sequence of events to a New York cop and a young man in a grey suit who thought police work was a matter of references, psychometric tests and the ability to successfully pass a pee test.

'Only Captain Opara can answer for his actions,' he said finally, knowing full well there and then that it was over.

Karl from the HR department was nodding sympathetically. I see, he seemed to be saying. Joseph wondered if he had recently read a book on empathising. Joseph knew he would never be able to convince these two white westerners that not every detective from Nigeria took dirty money, that not all of them were in the pay of the big Lagos gangsters, because that was exactly what they were thinking right now. He could tell this from the barely concealed contempt in the eyes of the veteran detective and the slowly dimming smile of the man from Human Resources.

4

Joseph pressed down firmly on the accelerator, keen to beat the lights before they turned red, so he could get back on the Cross Bronx Expressway, as far away from that damned office as possible. At the last moment, they changed and he was forced to hit the brake hard. He banged his palm against the steering wheel in frustration. It wasn't the long wait at the worst synchronised set of lights in the city that had him cursing, or even the parking ticket that had almost inevitably been waiting for him when he finally emerged from his wasted appointment with the New York Police Department. Instead it was the helplessness he felt about his current situation that had got to him, The interview he had just been through was a microcosm of his whole damned world. They were so understanding, so reasonable, so not telling him the truth. His test results and interview feedback would rest on file, they had assured him, and Joseph was perfectly free to apply again, once the small issue of his references had been tidied up. He had of course thanked them for their flexibility and for freeing the time they had spared in their busy schedules to see him. He promised them faithfully that he would solve the problem with the references and they would certainly see him again in the next round of applicants, some months down the line. However, he could tell they were not expecting to see his face again and, if he was forced to admit it, they were probably right in their assumption.

It was a bitter irony that his potential employers in the NYPD viewed him as someone who was so corrupt he had been forced to flee his country and was unable to obtain a reference from his own captain, when it was the reverse that was true. The New York Police Department would probably rather die than let such a man wear a badge and carry a gun, mingling with the gangsters and drug dealers on the streets of their fine city. Who knew what outrageous corruption might then ensue?

So that left Joseph driving a dilapidated taxi round the streets of the South Bronx, eking out a living as a cab driver, when he should have been solving crimes as a detective, and later he would have to go home and confront his own son over the business of concealing a weapon. As Eddie always said, it was a fucked-up world.

The dishes were washed and stacked on the draining board in an unruly pile. Joseph's attempt at a chilli had been passable enough and none of his fellow diners had complained or shown any sign of illness, which was always a relief. Four clean plates told their own story. Eddie had refilled his with seconds and polished off that plate, too. He probably hadn't eaten anything decent since his last meal at their apartment, thought Joseph.

The small room they were in doubled as kitchen-diner and living room. Joseph steered Eddie from the table into one of the two battered armchairs by the window, so they could look down at the lights of the city below. Yomi and his friend FJ were playing nearby. Only a year ago he had been known as Freddie, but then the boy had solemnly announced to Joseph that he should now be referred to only as FJ. This was not just his initials he had explained, but his true identity. Joseph had stifled a smile, nodded seriously and honoured the boy's wishes from then on. The retired cop from Jersey was a different matter however. He usually greeted Yomi's friend with the words 'say, if it isn't the artist formerly known as Freddie!' before chuckling manically at his own joke.

'We are gonna miss Lopez,' said FJ, sounding like a weary fifty-year-old man not a twelve-year-old boy. He was sitting cross-legged on the floor looking through a box of Yomi's baseball memorabilia. 'He even made maths interesting, at least some of the time. I tell you, man, that dude was way cooler than Geller when he stood in for him.'

The subject had inevitably come round to the murdered teacher, as Joseph had known it would.

'We sure are,' agreed Yomi, and he slouched down on the floor next to his friend. 'I wish he had taken football practice every week. He was nowhere near such a hard-ass. I'd say he was about the only nice one there.' Then he added quickly, 'Except Miss De Moyne,' and he looked guiltily up at his father, leaving Joseph to wonder why his son had been so quick to exclude Brigitte from his list of hated teachers.

'Oooh,' said FJ. 'Yomi loves Miss De Moyne.'

'No, I don't.'

'Yeah, you do,' and FJ began to sing, 'Yomi and Brigitte, sitting in a tree, K.I.S.S.I.N.G.!'

'Shut up,' Yomi whined, after FJ had spelled out the letters of the most terrifying word in his vocabulary. 'She's just interesting, that's all.'

'You mean she's fly.'

'No, I don't,' snapped Yomi.

'Fly?' asked Eddie. 'What in the name of ... is "fly"? Don't sound like a compliment to me to be compared to an insect.'

'Fly,' said FJ again, as if Eddie were hard of hearing. 'You know, "fly", like she's hot, you know what I'm saying.'

'I know what you saying, white boy,' answered Eddie, mocking FJ's gangsta mannerisms. 'You mean she's a doll. That's what you mean.'

'Whatever,' said FJ, who did not appreciate being mocked by his elders. Then he turned his attention back to Yomi. 'Yep, Brigitte's fly all right. Almost as fly as Laura Williams... Ow!' Joseph was shocked to see his son suddenly punch the other boy on the shoulder with some force.

'Cut it out, Yomi,' said Joseph.

'But he was saying stuff,' protested the boy.

'I don't care what he was saying, there's no need for hitting. Do you see me hitting Uncle Eddie when he teases me?'

'No.' The reply was sulky.

'Good job, too,' said Eddie with a smile. 'Or I'd kick your ass.'

'I'm going down to the frame,' announced FJ, as if the punch in the arm was the final straw. 'You coming?' The last words were a surly olive branch, like he knew he'd been a little out of line teasing his friend and he was trying to be conciliatory.

Yomi looked to his dad for approval.

'I don't know, Yomi. It's dark already.' Joseph meant he wasn't so keen on Yomi hanging round with the types who stood by the kid's climbing frame after dark.

'So?' asked his son as if that was an irrelevance.

'Can't keep a dog in its kennel for ever,

Joseph,' said Eddie.

'Who you calling a dog?' asked Yomi, but he seemed buoyed that the old man was on his side.

'One hour, you hear'?' ruled Joseph and the boys nodded their agreement before tearing off.

'He'll be okay,' said Eddie. 'He has to learn to survive round here on his own. You can't be with him every hour of the day.' Joseph knew Eddie was right, but it still filled him with dread to think of his son hanging out in the project at night. 'And that was nothing by the way. It wasn't really a fight. All boys have fights,' continued Eddie. 'Me? I grew up fighting. First my brothers, then my friends, I didn't have any time left to fight no enemies. You worry too much about Yomi. He's a good kid.'

'Oh yeah?' Joseph asked doubtfully.

'What? You been butting heads with him again? What is it this time?'

Joseph hadn't intended to discuss the subject with Eddie, but it had been eating away at him all day and he felt like he had to tell somebody. 'It's just, I found out he's been carrying a knife.'

'Get the fuck out... You serious?' Eddie shook his head. 'Yomi? Are you certain?'

'No.'

'Well then. What makes you think?'

Joseph explained about the toilet cistern and the blade that had been ditched there.

Eddie listened intently then he said, 'It could have been there, how long? Who knows?'

'Didn't look rusty to me and there was a fresh imprint from a boot just like Yomi's on the toilet seat.'

'But this is all circumstantial shit, Joseph, and you know it. How many other kids got feet the same size as him that could have climbed right up there and hid the knife before you came along? Wouldn't stand up in any court you and I been in. I mean, Jesus Christ this is Yomi we're talking about. You even talked to him about it yet?'

'Couldn't find the words,' admitted Joseph. 'I know, I know, I'll speak to him. I'm just choosing my moment. What with Hernando Lopez getting stabbed at the same time...'

'Surely you don't think Yomi had anything to with that?' asked Eddie.

'No, of course not. Anyhow, the police found the knife that killed Lopez. I meant, it just wasn't a good time to talk to him about it.'

'You're right,' conceded Eddie. 'Maybe he ditched the knife because he realised how it would look if he was caught carrying one, what with his teacher dying and all.'

'Or maybe he just didn't want the cops asking him difficult questions. What do you hear about the Lopez thing?' Joseph knew Eddie would have heard all about the stabbing. He always knew everything that happened in their neighbourhood.

'That it was most likely a kid from the school with a beef against his teacher.'

'It's what they are saying, but...'

'But what? If that's what they're saying, then it's most probably true. You were a cop, you know how it works. The word on the street is usually the way it is. You always got to listen to the street, Joseph. Proving it is the hard part. Me, I believe in Occam's Razor. The simplest solution is nearly always the best.'

'And I believe in an old Nigerian saying,' said Joseph. 'A tree does not move unless there is wind.'

'What's that supposed to mean?'

'It means a kid would have to have a real good reason to go into a school on his own after hours and knife his teacher to death. This wasn't some heat of the moment exchange, a row that ends with a knife being pulled and someone dying by accident. This was planned, premeditated murder and for what? The word on the street has yet to come up with one important thing.'

'What's that?'

'A motive.'

'Huh, believe me, Joseph, a lot of these kids they don't need a motive. It's all about respect with them. It's respect this and respect that, 'cept they don't know the true meaning of the word. If you look at them and they don't like it, you just disrespected them and they will kill you for it without giving it a thought. It's how they get their big-man reputations.'

'An interesting point,' said Joseph quietly. He was thinking about the gang tag on Eddie's door.

'Well, while you're mulling that one over, I'll pour us a drink. Looks like you could use an early one tonight, and the kids are out.'

Joseph didn't protest, so Eddie climbed out of his chair and shuffled over to the cabinet. He took out a couple of tumblers and poured two generous measures from the bottle of Bushmills he had brought with him. The two men savoured the whisky together for a while and, since Eddie had been so forthcoming with his opinion on Yomi, Joseph felt he could now be equally forthright.

'So, old man, are you going to tell me what you've gotten mixed up in, or are we going to carry on pretending that a gang hasn't made you its Public Enemy Number One?'

Eddie sighed wearily, took a little sip of his whisky and put the glass down on the rickety old table between them, then looked Joseph directly in the eye. He seemed to be contemplating how much to tell his friend. 'I keep telling you it ain't nothing. Just kids.' Joseph frowned and Eddie shrugged. 'Okay, I moved some of them on is all.'

'You moved them on, from where?'

'You know that little row of rundown lockups that backs on to George Washington Square?' Joseph nodded. He also knew that no one put cars in those garages any more as they were liable to be gone the next day. 'I noticed kids using it to store some stuff, so I spoke to them.'

'What kind of stuff?'

'The usual, TVs, DVDs, laptops. I watched 'em from one of the landings and I could see them unloading stuff from the lockup into a pick-up truck.'

'Why didn't you just call the cops?'

Eddie pretended to contemplate that for a

moment. 'Mmm let me see, ring the precinct and tell 'em that, amazingly, there is some stolen shit being offloaded out of a derelict garage in the Highbridge Project. I reckon their reply would be "you don't say? Call us back when that shit don't happen, maybe on a day without a Y in it". Even if they were interested they wouldn't come down here 'less they was mob-handed and tooled up like a S.W.A.T. team. You know they treat our neighbourhood like it's a no-go area these days. They've lost control of it.'

'Yet you go wandering down there on your own.'

'I had my reasons.'

'Are you gonna tell me then? Or do I got to guess?'

'You're finally talking like a New Yorker. How long's it been, two years?'

'Don't change the subject.'

'Okay,' and he sighed. 'Couple of days went by and I see this young boy, maybe thirteen, fourteen years old, standing outside that same lockup like he's a lookout or something, which means they're doing it again. Now police or no police, I'm not having that go on in our backyard, Joseph, not on my watch. But this kid, well what can I tell you, he's usually okay. I've known him and his family a long time. I watched him grow up round here and he ain't had a chance in hell. His father barely stuck around long enough to see him born before he was pulling down another sentence for peddling dope. His older brothers and sisters are all in gangs and his mother can't control any of them. I think she's about given up trying, but this kid, he's different. He ain't so bad and he's a great young football player, goes to the same school as Yomi incidentally.'

'What's his name?' asked Joseph.

'Jermaine Letts.'

'I've seen him play. He's good. He's two or three years older than Yomi but they've got the same coach.'

'That hard-assed Marine?'

'Coach Geller, that's the one. He seems to think Jermaine has the talent to go a long way.'

'Yeah, he could,' agreed Eddie. 'So anyhow I go right down there and I say to this kid: "I'm doing this as a courtesy to you, you go and see whoever has got you working here and you tell them to shift their shit out of the project like now. 'Cos if they don't I'm gonna call up some old police buddies who'll come down here and bust up the entire operation and all of you along with it".'

'And what did he say?'

'Not too much. He mostly took me at my word. The next day the whole stash had gone and all that's left of that lockup was a broken door hanging off its hinges.'

'But a day or so later you get a gang tag sprayed on your door.'

'Yeah.'

'And that don't worry you?'

'Joseph, I spent forty years busting up gangs, cracking heads and tangling with wise guys all over New Jersey. You always seem to forget that.'

'I hadn't forgotten it.'

Eddie seemed a little irritated by his friend, but he leaned forwards and poured him another measure of the Irish whisky anyway.

'You ever hear of Big Joey Moretti?'

'No.'

'Well, you sure as hell would have if you hadn't been a boy in Nigeria at the time. Hell I'm surprised they ain't heard of him even over there. He was one big, tough, hard wise-guy, a solider in the Patroni family. Anyway, he tangles with me this one time and, like he always does, he tells me he'd kick my sorry ass if I wasn't wearing a uniform. Well, I'd had just about enough of this wise-cracking asshole and that day, don't ask me why, something made me stop, turn round and take off my tunic. And you know what happened?'

'You kicked his ass.'

'I kicked his ass! In front of all of his crew, then I put my shirt back on and went for a beer with my partner. I tell you something, Joseph, that fight made me a legend in Jersey, a fucking legend, and I beat him fair ... well, mostly. I mean I banged his head off a fire hydrant but it ain't like we got rules about these things. There's no Marquis of Queens, you know what I'm saying. These were hard, hard men.'

'And your point is?'

'My point is you think I'm going to move out of my home 'cos some young, punk-ass kid who thinks he's a gangster sprays a fucked-up cartoon on my door. Get the fuck out of here!'

'I hear you, my friend and I understand, but be careful. Don't take this the wrong way, but you are the first to tell me you ain't quite the same as when you was a cop, physically I'm saying. I mean when was that fight? The sixties?'

'The sixties?' Eddie was incredulous. 'Shit no. It was the god dammed seventies.

Seventy-eight if you must know and I'm still the man I was then,' he snarled defensively. 'It's just my damn joints, that's all.' He was clearly taking offence and Joseph realised he had adopted the wrong approach. 'You think I'm some old man doesn't know what he's doing? How would you have made out without me when you came up against those dope-peddling, lowlifes from Claremont last year?'

Joseph had to concede he had a point. Eddie had helped him clear his friend Cyrus' name when he was framed for a shooting by a drug dealer. Without the former cop's experience and his contacts in the NYPD, things might not have worked out so well. For Cyrus or Joseph.

'Don't take offence, Eddie,' he urged.

'What do you expect me to take? You think you're the only one allowed to interfere when there's something going on you don't like? I told you not to mess with TJ and Baxter's crew and did you listen to me? No. Did you get yourself killed? No, not this time but you was lucky. It could easily have happened, so you ain't the guy to lecture me about being careful.'

'You're right, Eddie,' said Joseph simply. 'I apologise.'

'Apology accepted,' he said, but it sounded as if he was still far from happy.

Joseph tried to lighten the tone. 'So, what happened to Big Joey Moretti?'

'He got wacked,' said Eddie sourly. 'Shot in the head about five years later outside of a trattoria called Parmenteris.'

'Really? Why'd they kill him?'

'I hear he disrespected an older made guy,' said Eddie archly.

Joseph made a mental note never to tell a proud old man he is not what he used to be, because, even if it's true, he certainly doesn't want to hear it.

5

Joseph was standing, looking out across the school's sports field when he heard her call.

'Typical man,' said Brigitte, drawing alongside him. 'Watching sports all day.'

'Aren't you s'posed to be marking books or did you just give every body an A minus today, Miss De Moyne?' answered Joseph, smiling back at her.

Brigitte had changed into a sweatshirt and

jeans now the school day was at an end. The more casual look suited her and Joseph had to remind himself not to look too closely at her legs.

'I've been marking books for over an hour, thought I'd take a break and come join you.'

'How are you, Brigitte?' He meant since the death of her friend and colleague, and she understood.

'What are you gonna do?' she asked. 'Gotta keep going, life goes on, I guess,' she offered uncertainly, and she looked out onto the sports field at the disorderly clump of boys all trying to dive onto the same foul ball, 'Are we winning?'

'This is just practice.' He gestured towards the man in his mid forties who was standing in amongst the boys, bellowing instructions. 'Coach Geller's instilling a little discipline.'

'That sounds like the clean-Marine,' she said.

Geller made no secret of his Marine Corps background, revelled in it in fact, right down to the number-one, buzz-cut style he always sported, which left little more than a thin, fuzzy layer of hair on the top of his head. The man may have retired from 'the Corps', as he called it, but Joseph felt his heart was still very much on the parade ground.

'So why are you here?' asked Brigitte. 'If it's just practice.'

'I'm a cab driver remember,' he smiled. 'Yomi's personal cab driver. I'm taking him home afterwards. Plus I get to drop a couple of his friends on the way, too.'

Brigitte smiled. 'That's nice. I'll bet he thinks he has the coolest dad around.'

'I'd say that's unlikely. Anyway I'm not the only one.' Joseph raised a hand and received a slow, hesitant wave across the pitch in return from Merve Williams. The last time he had seen the big man with his youngest daughter Laura they had been standing outside the school and she had been in tears. Now they were watching her brother Chris go through his paces with some of the older kids.

Laura was almost exactly the same age as Yomi, and Joseph had assumed they were still friends, but for some reason his son had pretty much blanked the girl when they had all arrived at the field together. Joseph had virtually forced him to say hello when she had said, 'Hi, Yomi.'

Laura was probably bored out of her mind watching this display, thought Joseph, but her father seemed deeply interested in the training session. Coach Geller had boys from three different age groups all practising moves together in different quarters of the playing field. They watched as the coach put the boys through their paces. Geller was a big man with a barrel chest that bulged out against a faded, old, military-issue tracksuit in army green. His legs were as muscular as his torso, but his face was lined and ageing and Joseph had never seen it once crack into a smile while scrutinising his charges on the football field.

Philip Geller liked to tell the boys he believed in three things, discipline, discipline, discipline. Yomi disliked Geller for his strictness, and Joseph privately held his own doubts as to whether a retired Marine Corps non-commissioned officer was the right man to be teaching twelve-year-olds how to play football. Weren't they supposed to still be enjoying the game at that age instead of being bawled at by Sergeant Rock? The school probably felt a man like Geller was needed to keep control of their team and knock some of the older boys into shape. Like most American schools, Antoinette Irving Junior High took its football very seriously.

The boys were all gathered round the coach now in a respectful semi circle, some of them panting for breath from the exertion of the latest moves he'd put them through. Yomi was out there, too, bent double with his hands on his knees. Even from the touchline, Joseph could clearly make out most of Coach Geller's exhortations to work as a unit, get in there and scrap for your buddies, hold the line and break hard, trample the other guys and don't give them a second chance.

To Joseph it all sounded a bit too much like a military campaign. When he was Yomi's age, he'd have been kicking a battered old football round the side streets of Lagos with his friend Cyrus, dreaming of playing for the national side, the Super Eagles. There were no coaches or tactics, no training runs or lifting weights, and no referee. The goal would have been an irregular chalk line, drawn onto the back wall of an old garage. Things had certainly changed since he was a kid.

Geller suddenly stopped speaking and looked up just as a silver Honda Accord flashed past them all. It was heading down the dirt track at the side of the football field at an improbable speed. There was a harsh scraping sound as the tyres spun against the loose gravel and everyone turned to see the cause of the disturbance. The driver sounded the horn a couple of times. Joseph turned towards the commotion in time to see a flash of blonde hair and an imperious wave from the driver's seat.

'Who was that?' he asked.

Brigitte sighed and spoke low so as not to be overheard. 'That shy and retiring figure is Macy Williams, Merve William's eldest, driving her daddy's old hatchback, since he got him himself a new one. I used to teach her. Like most of the seventeen year olds round here she gets her manners from reruns of Jerry Springer and her values from MTV.' Joseph laughed. 'I'm not joking. I once asked a classroom full of thirteen year olds to name a good role model and straightaway one of the girls said Britney Spears. When I asked her why she said, and I'm quoting here, "cos she does what she wants and don't take no shit from nobody, uh-huh". I thought she was going to call me "girlfriend". I had to explain it's a little harder to live like that if you don't have a bank account with several zeros, but I fear my words may have fallen on stony ground.'

On the pitch in front of him the coach had recommended his team talk.

'Maybe they just don't understand things at that age,' offered Joseph.

But Brigitte would not be placated. 'The girls in this school don't want to be Hilary

Clinton or Condoleezza Rice, they want to be J-Lo or Lindsay Lohan. The female role models of today are pop-trash, teen-queens, stepping out of cars with no panties on and not caring a damn when their tushies are posted all over the Internet afterwards.'

'And who did you want to be when you were fourteen years old, Brigitte? Nancy Reagan? Mother Theresa? Dian Fossey, hanging out with the gorillas in the jungle?'

She blushed a little. 'Point taken.'

'No, come on, I'm curious.'

'Well, if you must know I wanted to be Meryl Streep.'

'Really?'

'Passionately. I used to imagine myself accepting an Oscar for some worthy film role set in Africa or Poland.'

'What a serious little girl you were. Nothing more frivolous than that?'

'Well, I'll admit to one if you'll tell me yours.'

'Deal.'

'When I was thirteen I wanted to be Tiffany.' And she giggled, which Joseph couldn't help but find endearing.

'That girl who sang in shopping malls? We even got her on the TV in Lagos.'

'That's the one. I used to stand in front of

the mirror for hours singing into my hair-brush.'

'And what happened to those ambitions of fame?'

She pulled a face. 'Turns out I can't sing and I can't act.'

'Hollywood's loss was Antoinette Irving's gain.'

'If you say "those that can do, and those that can't teach", I swear I will hit you, Joseph Soyinka.'

'I would never dream of it. I think teaching's a fine thing to do.'

'You really mean that, don't you?' She seemed impressed.

'Of course. When Yomi comes home from your class he tells me what he's been learning. It's good to hear he takes it all in and it proves you make a difference.'

'Thank you, that's nice to know,' she said. 'So who did you want to be then, Joseph?'

'When I was a boy in Lagos?'

'Uh-huh.'

'Well, I'm not sure I can remember.'

'Not fair.' She said it like she was a child again. 'I showed you mine, so you got to show me yours.'

'Since you put it like that.'

'Go on.'

Before Joseph could answer, their attention was diverted by the sound of another vehicle. This time it was a police squad car that was easing its way along the same dirt track Macy Williams had just shot down in her pick-up. It was heading steadily towards them and everybody stopped to watch its progress, including Coach Geller and all of his charges. The car rolled to a standstill by the touchline and two uniformed officers climbed out. One of the cops opened the rear door and out stepped none other than Assistant Chief McCavity. The three of them walked straight out onto the football field, right up to Coach Geller and the surrounding huddle of boys. There was a short, muffled conversation that Joseph could not make out, then the officers broke away from the group and began to return to their car. This time they had a boy with them, he was about fourteen years old and still dressed in his football kit, the only addition to it being the handcuffs that were keeping his hands clasped tightly together behind him.

The cops were clearly taking no chances. They weren't going to let him change his clothes and made sure they stood either side of the youngster, holding him firmly by the arms so he couldn't make a run for it as he was led to their car. McCavity led the way, the two officers followed behind and, as the figure they were escorting drew nearer, he was instantly recognisable to Joseph. The boy was tall and well built for his age, with the muscles of a young man already honed from hours of incessant football practice. The boy's hair was shaved short but, unlike Coach Geller's, his haircut spoke more of the street than an institution like the army. He may have resembled a man physically but the confusion and hurt in his eyes was still that of a child. As he was led away, it was clear to Joseph that the boy was terrified.

'Talk of the devil,' Joseph said to himself

'What?' asked Brigitte, as she watched the police dragging the boy along.

'That's Jermaine Letts, isn't it?'

'Sure is.'

One of the cops pressed Jermaine's head down so he was bent forwards and bundled into the back of the squad car. This time, McCavity rode up front, leaving the burliest male officer to travel in the back with the boy. Joseph wondered why she had chosen a marked squad car and uniformed officers for the arrest, instead of an unmarked vehicle and plainclothes detectives. He knew McCavity never did anything without a reason.

Then he realised, from the stunned looks on the faces of the children and the handful of parents scattered along the touchline, that she had opted for this approach deliberately. No one was going to forget this spectacle in a hurry. They were more likely to remember McCavity next time she was on the news, possibly even recall her years from now when she was canvassing their vote for some public office. The memory of the squad car parked on the edge of the football field, the cops with their batons and guns, the flame-haired detective in the power suit was so much more effective than a quiet and anonymous arrest at Jermaine Letts' family home. McCavity certainly knew how to make an entrance.

Brigitte said, 'You don't think?'

'That Jermaine is responsible for the killing of Hernando Lopez? I don't know but I doubt they would drive out all this way to pick him up if he had just robbed the charity box from his church, do you?'

'Nope,' she said glumly. 'And I've heard he does have gang links.'

'So I hear,' said Joseph. 'It's a small world.'

'What do you mean?' she asked.

'Nothing,' he said.

Coach Geller had broken up the training session as soon as the police car disappeared. He traipsed off the pitch right by Joseph and Brigitte, to be met by a small cluster of curious parents filled with questions. He told them what he knew. 'I don't suppose it's a state secret that Jermaine Letts has just got himself arrested for the murder of Hernando Lopez.' The coach had then made it clear where his own sympathies lay. 'There's no helping some of these kids,' he told anybody that would listen, 'might as well take 'em straight from the womb and stick 'em in an eight-by-five cell. They are going to wind up in the prison yard one day anyhow. It's either that or drown them at birth.' Geller must have spotted the look Joseph gave him. 'What?' he challenged. 'Say it isn't so? I ain't saying it's not sad, but Jermaine Letts' daddy is in a state correctional facility right now. He's a dope fiend, a no-good pothead pusher. How long you think it will be before his son joins him there, with or without what happened to Lopez, that poor, sorry son-of-a-bitch. They say he suffered before he died and I for one believe in an eye for an eye.'

There were murmurs of agreement from about half of the assembled parents. The others chose to keep their own counsel. One or two looked at the ground.

Joseph didn't bother to argue. Geller was the stuff lynch mobs were made of. Once he had an idea in his head there was no shaking it. Maybe he was right. Perhaps Jermaine Letts never had a chance from the day he was born. Maybe he did kill his teacher and now he would get what he deserved, but maybe, just maybe, he had nothing to do with it at all.

Once Yomi was showered and changed, he traipsed out to meet his father with his friends. On the way home, FJ and the other guys were full of fevered speculation about Jermaine Letts and his future. Mostly it centred around whether he was capable of 'sticking' his teacher like that and, if so, where he would end up once the courts found him guilty. The consensus seemed to be that he was more than capable of such an act and now he was going to go to prison for the rest of his natural life. FJ ventured that he might be lucky and finally be freed back into society when he was a stooped and wrinkly old man. So much for Eddie's theory that Jermaine was a good kid, thought Joseph. Yomi's friends didn't seem to think the older boy was worth a light.

Despite the shock of Jermaine's arrest and the excited chattering of the other boys, Yomi himself was uncharacteristically quiet. When his friends had all been dropped at their respective homes, Joseph asked, 'Are you okay, son?'

'Yeah.' Yomi was quiet for a time, then he said, 'Everybody says Jermaine Letts is a bad kid, but he's not.'

'Really?' It seemed a strange thing to say about the chief suspect in a homicide.

'He's tough but he's not a bully. He protects his younger brother from the bigger kids and he looks out for people.'

'Yomi, are you upset because they arrested this boy?'

Yomi just shrugged. 'It's not that.' Then he corrected himself *'Not just* that, I mean.'

'Then what is it?'

'You know you always said if I was in trouble I could come talk to you, no matter what?'

Joseph got the distinct impression he was going to regret those words and sooner rather than later. 'Yes.'

'Well, I'm in trouble now.'

'What kind of trouble?'

Yomi took a long time to answer his father and Joseph had to tell himself to count to ten before he flew off the handle. He knew Apara would have told him not to push too hard. Let the boy speak in his own good time and it will all come out eventually, she would reason. Instead Yomi just stared out of the cab window as a street full of rundown stores with metal shutters or steel cages over their shabby windows rolled by outside.

Finally he spoke. 'That knife the cops found in Lopez's classroom.' He said it hesitantly and Joseph realised he was holding his breath now. 'They're gonna find my prints all over it.'

6

Joseph did not sleep well that night, even by his usual standards. He eventually gave up entirely before the first white light of an early winter morning peeped through the drapes in his tiny bedroom. Instead he walked out into the living room and sat down heavily in his ancient armchair, waiting for the sun to come up over the projects at the start of another day. He'd been up for nearly two hours before Yomi emerged groggily from his room to begin the school day. The pair of them drove to Antoinette Irving Junior High in silence. There wasn't much left to say. It had all been said the night before.

Joseph had tried not to fly off the handle, but the row that began in the cab on the way home from football practice the night before had continued in their apartment. Joseph had demanded to know how his son's fingerprints could possibly be found on a murder weapon.

'People were saying that it was Jermaine's knife the police found but I didn't know for sure,' he said sadly. 'Until they took him away.'

'That doesn't answer my question, Yomi. How did your prints get on it?'

It was killing Yomi to give his father the truth. 'He took it from me.'

Joseph took a moment to understand what his son was saying, 'You mean it was your knife?'

'Yes.'

'And Jermaine Letts stole it from you?'

'No.'

'Well, what then?' Joseph's fear was beginning to turn to anger. 'You're not making any sense.'

'He took it from me because he said I was

78

too young to be carrying a knife.'

Joseph felt like he'd been punched in the gut. He sat down opposite his son and tried to calm his growing rage. 'Well, Jermaine was right. What in hell were you doing with a knife, Yomi? You're twelve years old. I didn't bring you up to carry one, damn it!'

'Dad, it's for protection. Everybody carries a blade.'

'No, they don't. Not at your age.' Joseph said it adamantly, but he was now no longer sure about this.

'They do, they do.' Yomi was raising his voice now, teenage frustration making him angry at his father. 'You don't understand. You're nobody unless they know you're carrying. They've got to know or they'll beat you bad. This is the only way I can keep the gangs off my back. Oh, you don't get it!' He was shouting now and Joseph was taken aback. He expected shame and guilt from his son, not this. He was looking for understanding, apologies and contrition. Instead he was getting defiance from a misguided twelve year old, who couldn't see that it was wrong to carry a knife. And this particular twelve year old was his own son.

'So, you carry a knife to protect you from the older boys?'

'Yes.'

'And yet an older boy comes along and takes it off you with ease, just like that. What if he'd stabbed you with it, Yomi? What then?'

'It wasn't like that. Jermaine's a good guy. They all say he isn't, but he is. He's the best football player in his year and I'm one of the best in mine, so there's respect.' That word again, thought Joseph, the one they bandy around all the time without remotely understanding its meaning. 'He saw me showing my knife to a couple of the girls and he told me I shouldn't be carrying at my age. Then he just took it, but he didn't make me look bad in front of them and he didn't kick me around or nothing.'

'Well, that's okay then,' said Joseph with heavy sarcasm, for in truth he was struggling to find the right words to make his son understand. 'And you just accepted what he said?'

'Yes.'

'And that was the end of the matter, was it? You agreed with Jermaine's appraisal, since you respect this older boy so much?'

Yomi was squirming a little. 'I guess.'

'So you didn't go right out and buy a new knife?'

Yomi hesitated for just a second and his father could see the lie in his eyes even before he spoke.

'No.'

Joseph walked over to the cupboard where he kept the bottle of whisky and the glass tumblers. He opened the little drawer above the bottle and slid his hand in till he found what he was looking for. As Yomi watched him, Joseph drew out a duster and unwrapped it. In the middle of the cloth was the lock knife Joseph had fished out of the cistern at Antoinette Irving. Yomi seemed to wilt visibly in front of him.

When Joseph spoke he was having difficulty containing his anger. 'Yomi, so help me I have never ever raised a hand to you but if you lie to me now I don't know what I will do. I found this knife in the school bathroom the day that Mr Lopez was stabbed. Is it yours?'

Yomi ducked his head, unable to look his father directly in the eye and when he finally admitted it the word was barely audible 'yes'.

Joseph let out a deep breath. 'How could you do this, Yomi? After all the times we have talked about what it means to be a man, to do the right thing, not follow your stupid friends when they do all the stuff that gets them into trouble. There's no winner in a knife fight. What happens if you don't get stabbed? You kill the other boy, that's what. You want to go to jail for the rest of your life? How could you do it?'

'It's not my fault!' Yomi shouted. 'I didn't ask to come here. You brought me to this shitty place when Mom died. You know how hard it is for me? Every day I go to that school I don't know who's going to try and give me a beating. Every day! You told me we were going to America and you'd be a cop again and we'd have a nice place to live. That's what you said. Instead you drive a cab and we've got nothing. We live in these horrible rooms in this bad place and I have to carry a blade so I don't get stabbed by some other kid. It's all your fault! What do you want from me?'

Joseph was rocked by his son's response. He could never get beyond the idea that any boy who carried a knife was either a fool, a thug or both but he couldn't deny that everything his son had just said to him was true. He had promised Yomi a new and better life in America then singularly failed to provide it. The job driving a cab, the crumbling apartment, the school so rough they were talking about installing metal detectors so no more teachers or pupils would be murdered there. All of this was his fault because he had trusted Captain Opara and he had stuck to his fine principles, right up until the point when they had killed Yomi's mother and driven him and his son out of the country. Right now he couldn't help thinking that if he had only taken the damned dirty money when it had been offered to him, he would still be living in Lagos in his nice home with his beautiful wife. He certainly wouldn't be having this conversation with his son about carrying a knife.

'Yomi,' said Joseph quietly when his son's tirade had finally ceased. 'Just go to your room.'

It had been another frustrating day of delays on the Cross Bronx Expressway. Joseph's nerves had been shattered by a symphony of car horns, pointlessly sounded, as if their repetition would magically clear the way up ahead and set the traffic moving on its way again.

When he was finally free of the gridlock and back in the tenements of the South Bronx, he managed to get a couple of fares back to back but it was to be a temporary respite. Something had suddenly blown in the engine and steam started to hiss out from beneath the bonnet of the cab. Cursing his luck, Joseph pulled over, took a rag from the glove box and went round to the front of the Crown Victoria. He knew he should let the ancient radiator cool down before he did anything but he was way behind schedule, so he pressed the rag against the cap and turned it. He was rewarded by a gush of steam followed by a short spurt of piping-hot water that bubbled up onto his hand before he could move it away. Passers-by heard the language of a man who truly felt as if life was pushing him to the brink. Joseph cursed the car, the city he lived in and his own stupidity in that order. Then he willed himself to calm down.

He would get the old cab looked at by Selwyn down at Wrays' garage just as soon as he could. In the meantime, the problem with the radiator could be fixed. All he needed was water. He told himself it could have been far worse and he wandered away to find a Korean store whose owner sold him two litres of mineral water for the same price of a cold glass of beer down at the Impala. As he trudged back to the cab, he used the time to go over the events of the previous night.

Jermaine Letts may not have been a bad kid

at heart but he was still the prime suspect in a murder investigation, one which might soon implicate his own son. Yomi had admitted to handling the murder weapon, to his father if not yet the police, and now Joseph was torn. Should he go to the cops himself and explain what had happened with the knife, in the hope it might go easier for Yomi in the long run, or should he sit tight hoping the police might never follow up on the other prints, particularly if they had already wrung a confession out of Jermaine Letts. He had to admit he did not relish the idea of turning in his own son. He had witnessed first hand the suspicion that could be created within the NYPD if they failed to fully comprehend a situation. His own recent job interview had been a prime illustration of that.

Joseph's worries were compounded by the gang tag sprayed on Eddie's door. The old man had already admitted to a run-in with Jermaine Letts. If the boy really was a gang leader, capable of murder over the most trivial of grievances then Eddie could be in grave danger. How many more members of Jermaine Letts' gang would hope to gain a reputation by stabbing a retired policeman for no other reason than he was in their way?

Joseph was bitterly cold by the time he

returned to his car. The radiator had been the last warm thing in New York but it had cooled down by now and it swallowed the water gratefully. A car must really be on its last legs for it to overheat in wintertime, thought Joseph, but at least he was back on his way again now. There was a reason for his urgency. He had to get a couple more fares in and earn some more precious dollars before he picked Yomi up from school and dropped him back at the apartment. He would have to cook them both a meal before leaving Yomi with Eddie for a couple of hours. Then he had to go out once more.

He would lie to his son. He had done it before and he would do it again for there was nothing to be gained right now by telling him the truth. He didn't like doing it but he could see no good reason to tell Yomi he was meeting Brigitte De Moyne that evening. Life with his son was difficult enough right now without any additional complication.

Brigitte was going to be mad at him, for he was over half an hour late and he had still not reached her apartment. Joseph had never made up the time he lost getting the cab back on the road. He'd have called ahead but the power light on his mobile had blinked its last half an hour ago then expired, along with the battery. He'd charged it fully the night before, so it looked like here was another thing that was in need of repair. When life's really got it in for you, thought Joseph, your troubles come in multitudes.

He had been looking forward to tonight though. It was only going to be a couple of hours in her company but that was something, a relief from the daily grind. He remembered their agreement, their pact to keep it a secret. She had said it would be all right as long as no one else knew and he had readily agreed. Throughout the course of a long and stressful day, he periodically remembered he would soon be seeing her and been surprised by how much he was looking forward to it.

7

Brigitte was in the moment, mind entirely concentrated on the act. Joseph watched her now and she hardly noticed when a single, unruly lock of her hair broke loose and tumbled down over her forehead. Oblivious, her eyes narrowed and her mouth opened to form a perfect letter O as she let her breath out in a shallow gasp, took in another then held it. She stretched her arms out in front of her.

Brigitte's grip on the gun was too tight, and it caused her hand to tremble. She forced herself to ease it, adjusted her stance and bit her bottom lip hard as she aimed her weapon at the mugger.

'Do it,' urged Joseph and Brigitte obeyed, squeezing the trigger then bracing herself for the recoil as the automatic pistol fired and sent a bullet straight into the mugger's chest. Brigitte rocked back on her heels slightly but rode the recoil and Joseph watched as the mugger came towards them at speed.

Brigitte calmly placed the gun down on the table in front of her. The paper target, with the scowling face of a criminal etched onto it, was propelled along on a backboard attached to a mechanised pulley that hung down from the roof. It pulled up abruptly just over the table and Joseph reached out and grabbed it. They both peered at the damage Brigitte's six shots had inflicted. 'Not bad,' he said approvingly. 'Remind me never to have a disagreement with you.' There were distinct holes in the mugger's chest, shoulder, stomach and left cheek and, with one shot, Brigitte had parted his hair. The sixth had gone wide of the mark but she was clearly making progress. She seemed happy and there was something undeniably cathartic about pumping bullets into a paper target that represented the asshole who knocked you to the ground and stole your stuff.

'Is he dead?' she asked dryly

'I'd say he's robbed his last grandma, wouldn't you?'

Brigitte nodded. 'Good,' she said it firmly, satisfied by her new-found marksmanship.

'Careful you don't turn into Charles Bronson.'

'I would never have dreamed of owning a gun before,' she admitted. 'But having a .38 pushed into your face makes you rethink your stance on life and criminals.'

Brigitte had her car jacked from an underground car park at her friend's apartment block and she'd been understandably traumatised by the experience. The police told her the mugger had probably been waiting some time until a vulnerable, female victim came along. As soon as she opened the car door, he had come out of nowhere. She freely admitted she had not heard or seen a thing before he was at her side. The guy had pulled a gun, ordering her to cooperate and cautioning her not to scream for help. He had torn the handbag from her arm, before climbing into Brigitte's car and tearing out of the car park in it at speed. The last thing she saw was the thin, wooden exit barrier being obliterated by her Mazda as it careered through without stopping.

'I do know what you mean,' said Joseph. 'I've been shot at and the last thing in my mind right then was whether the guy had a good start in life or if he should be given a second chance by society. You shoot back and worry about it later, pure and simple, and you can't aim to wound, it's not possible. You hit him in the chest and if he happens to still be breathing afterwards then that's fine, but in the heat of the moment it's you or him.'

'And it's not going to be me again,' she promised.

Joseph had known many victims of crime. Guilt, shame and feelings of inadequacy were commonplace among them. They tended to constantly question whether they could have done more to prevent their attack taking place, not realising they were simply the victims of experienced professional villains.

'I tell you, Joseph, if I ever see that guy

again, I won't be looking to wound him.'

'You are gonna hate me for saying this, Brigitte, but in many ways you were lucky.'

She shot him an angry look.

'Think about it; you weren't seriously injured, you could have been killed or raped. All he took was your handbag and your car. The credit cards are covered, and so is the Mazda. I'm not saying you've got to be happy about it but...'

'It could have been worse, I know. It's just...' She didn't have to explain further. The frustration of being a victim with no recourse to justice, no chance to avenge, well, he knew that feeling more than she would ever know. Right now, she needed the sense of power and safety a gun afforded her. She had pleaded with him to teach her how to shoot. Joseph had plenty of experience with guns from his time in Lagos, so, a little reluctantly at first, he had agreed to take her to the range and show her what he knew. He realised there was a certain irony in teaching Brigitte how to become proficient with a gun the day after he had torn into his son for carrying a knife.

The sessions on the range had been surprisingly enjoyable. It had been satisfying to pass on his expertise and she was a willing pupil. She looked good too, having changed into jeans and a T-shirt before they left her apartment. She had even asked him, 'How do I look?'

'Good,' he'd told her. 'It suits you,' and it did, but not as much as the tight, latex vest top showing off Brigitte's ample curves. Stop thinking like that, Joseph, he told himself.

'Since you taught me how to shoot up the bad guys, I guess I owe you a cup of coffee.'

'I ought to be going really. I'm supposed to be meeting up with Eddie.'

'That the old cop you told me about?'

'That's the one.'

'How come you two are such buddies anyhow?'

He took a while to answer her, wondering how to explain their friendship, founded as it was on tragedy and shared loss. 'His wife died some time back. I guess we have that in common.' As he said this, Brigitte instinctively stretched out her arm, placed her hand on his shoulder and squeezed it. The gesture had been an entirely natural one for her. It was meant to convey support, but it made Joseph feel immediately uncomfortable in a way he would have struggled to explain. Perhaps it was a form of guilt that his reward for admitting to the loneliness of widowhood was the physical touch of another woman. He knew it wasn't Brigitte's fault. She had a kind heart, but something prevented him from enjoying her touch. He deliberately made the rest of his explanation more mundane. 'We play chess, drink a little whisky. Not too much,' he added quickly. 'Mostly we just talk but he's not so good in the kitchen so he has dinner with us from time to time.'

'It's nice of you to cook for him like that.'

'Eddie's a good neighbour. He takes Yomi for me when I need it, he's looking after him right now as a matter of fact.'

'Then I won't keep you long, just one cup of coffee,' she said before adding, 'Does anybody ever cook for you, Joseph?'

'Not really.'

'Then maybe I will one day.'

Joseph hesitated for a moment before answering. 'That'd be nice,' he managed to say, but he knew something was making him hold back. There was no doubt Brigitte was an attractive woman. It wasn't like he hadn't noticed and it wasn't as if she hadn't noticed him noticing. She didn't seem to mind. Apara had been gone two years now but somehow he still wasn't quite ready for more than friendship with this attractive teacher and he couldn't exactly explain why, not even to himself. 'You can bring Yomi too, of course,' she said quickly, turning it back into a non-date, and then she took her hand away.

'Thanks,' he said, but he did not press her to name the day.

They were on a non-date already. This was their fourth trip to the shooting gallery. He justified teaching her lethal force because it made her feel better and he knew she would have gone off and bought a weapon anyway, even without his help. If there was one thing scarier than Brigitte with a gun, it was Brigitte with a gun she didn't know how to use.

They took their coffee at the diner across the street. Like a lot of places in the South Bronx that wasn't either a chain or a franchise, it was crumbling and weather-beaten, with not enough cash left over from the day's takings to put any aside for refurbishment. It was one of those old-fashioned places with walls painted ketchup red, chrome on the edge of every table and counter top and little, individual juke boxes for each customer. The place was probably created with young couples in mind, the kind who share fries and a burger then slot

94

the last of their dimes into the juke box so it can play a song they are convinced has been written about them. The short-order chef had a tiny, white hat made of card that matched his apron and the waitress wore a skirt way too short for her advancing years. She greeted them with a forced cheeriness.

'Hi there, welcome to Lacey's Diner. What can I get you guys today?' she asked then proceeded to go through all of the specials before they had any opportunity to interrupt her. She recited the whole list by rote, like an actress who has been playing the same part on Broadway for way too many performances. She still knew all of her lines, but any enthusiasm she might once have had for the part had long since died.

'Er ... just coffee please,' he told her when she was finally done.

The waitress failed to hide her disappointment and sauntered away to fetch the percolator.

'I keep thinking about Jermaine Letts,' said Brigitte when their coffee was finally poured. 'Being led away in handcuffs like that in front of everybody.'

'Do you think he did it?' asked Joseph, taking a sip and realising his coffee was almost cold already.

'Killed Hernando, truthfully?' She seemed to be mulling the idea over. 'I don't know but the police seem to think he did.'

'You said he had gang links?'

'Through his family,' she nodded, 'and he's been in trouble before. Last year he stole a computer console, or at least everybody says it was him. I guess he was boasting about it to his friends. The police heard something about it and they took his prints but they couldn't pin that one on him. No proof. Jermaine's an older boy whose been kept back a year. He shouldn't even be at school. It wouldn't surprise me at all if he was in a gang.'

'What makes the police so sure it was Jermaine who stabbed Hernando Lopez?'

'They're not saying much,' answered Brigitte in hushed tones, 'but it seems Hernando was killed by the knife he took from that boy in class. It turns out that boy was Jermaine. Since they already had his prints on file, I guess it won't be too hard for the police to get a match.'

And why did Jermaine have a knife in the first place, thought Joseph, because he took it off my son. Trying to do a good deed for once and look where it had got him. Joseph told himself he was probably being naive. He didn't really know Jermaine Letts at all, except by reputation as a school football player. He only had Eddie's character reference to go on and the fact that Yomi respected the older boy, but his son's values were a little messed up right now and the old cop could easily have been wrong about the youngster he'd watched grow up. Jermaine would not be the first kid to lose his way and ruin his life before it had even begun.

Joseph had been thinking about the stabbing of Hernando Lopez a lot lately, more so now that he knew his son's knife was the murder weapon. He couldn't help himself and it wasn't just old-fashioned professional curiosity. He dreaded the day the police called to ask him if he knew anything about his son owning the knife that caused Lopez's death. Why should Jermaine not answer truthfully when asked where he got the knife from? 'There is one aspect to this killing that I can't quite understand,' he told her.

'What's that?'

'Don't you think it's odd that Hernando Lopez locked himself in his classroom only to bleed to death like that?'

'Maybe,' she said uncertainly. 'I've been trying not to think about it if I'm honest. I guess he was trying to protect himself from his attacker.'

'Possibly, but there comes a point when you know you've got to get out of there. Think about it, he had no mobile phone, he's in urgent need of medical assistance, he's bleeding badly...'

Brigitte pulled a face like she really didn't want to contemplate the grim fate of poor Hernando any further but she said, 'Perhaps he didn't realise. How close he was to death, I mean. The knife could've struck an artery.'

'It's possible, I suppose,' he conceded, though he doubted it very much. He didn't want to explain to Brigitte that if the knife had severed an artery there would have been a whole lot more blood at the scene. It would have been everywhere and could have even hit the ceiling. 'But if it did take a while, do you think his killer really stood outside the door all that time watching Lopez bleed to death through the window? Particularly when the first instinct of most people would have been to get the hell out of there before they were discovered. That would be one cold-blooded S.O.B. and I wouldn't have thought a fourteen-year-old...'

'I'm not sure I want to contemplate that right now.'

'Okay, but what would you do in his

shoes? You've just been stabbed, you need help, what would you do?'

'I don't know.' Her forehead creased into a frown. 'I see what you mean about him locking himself in like that, it is a little strange, but I can't see how else it could have happened. It's not as if anybody left through the window, they only open a little way to let in air. They are specifically designed to prevent students from jumping through them or throwing anyone else out.'

'Someone else could have locked the door and left him to die in there. Maybe he wasn't trying to lock himself in, perhaps he was trying to get out.'

'I see where you are going with, but that's just not possible. There are only three sets of keys to those classrooms. The principal has one, which I assume he leant to Hernando so he could work late on his marking, that's not uncommon by the way. I've borrowed keys when I've been marking tests. Ardo, the janitor, has a set and the master keys are kept in the school safe.'

'Could anybody have got access to the master set?'

'I don't see how.'

'What about borrowing the keys from Decker and cutting a new set?'

'Not that easy, I'm afraid, you need a certificate to get those kind of keys cut, it's illegal otherwise.'

'Illegal but not impossible. When you borrowed keys from Decker in the past, did you get to keep them overnight? I'm assuming you must do, otherwise you couldn't lock up the school.'

'Yes, overnight, yeah,' she admitted a little defensively, 'but could you go easy on the questions please, Joseph? I'm starting to feel like a suspect here.'

'Sorry,' he said. 'I guess old habits die hard.'

'I guess they do. You know, it's funny, when I first met you it never crossed my mind you might have been a cop but once you told me it all kind of made sense.'

'Really, how so?'

'The analytical mind, always looking at things from different angles, questioning everything. You like to get to the bottom of stuff, find out how people tick. You do it with me sometimes.'

'Do I?' he was genuinely surprised. 'I'm sorry.'

'Don't be. It's okay.' She smiled at him. 'I mean, I don't have to tell you anything I don't want to, right.'

'Of course.'

'A girl's gotta keep some mystery.' She drained her coffee cup then said, 'Just remember, though, Detective Soyinka, that sometimes, as folk are fond of saying round these parts, shit just happens. There's no explanation, no great profound mystery, it just occurs for no great reason we can see and we have to live with it.'

'Fair point,' he conceded, but he was far from convinced. Joseph knew too much about human nature to go along with that notion.

'It's like the gang thing,' continued Brigitte. 'They have their own sub culture, their own rules that we don't always get.'

'You know much about these gangs I keep hearing about?' he asked.

'Joseph, I'm a junior high school teacher...'

'Yeah, stupid question, sorry.' How could she know about such matters, he reasoned?

'...you don't understand. I'm a junior high school teacher, of course I know about the gangs. I could practically write my doctorate on the subject. Hell, I could go and teach a class on gangs at Yale, maybe I will. Got to be better money. I could be Professor of Homeys with a fellowship in "dissing".' He was laughing along with her now. 'I see gang culture every time I walk through the front door of the school.'

Joseph glanced at his watch. He would be a little late, but Brigitte's first-hand knowledge of the gangs intrigued him. 'Then enlighten me. I'm curious about it.'

'Why?'

'I have a son,' he said, by way of explanation, not wanting to tell her about the tag on Eddie's door. 'I worry about these things.' He waved the waitress over and she refilled their coffee cups. 'So who are these gangs?'

'There's a whole bunch of them. Some are based on the two big gangs, the Crips and the Bloods. They have hundreds of thousands of members all over America but the kids aren't usually directly affiliated to them.'

'How do you mean?'

'The small gangs are like those little-league baseball sides that name themselves after the Mets or the Yankees but aren't really anything to do with the big clubs. They just model themselves on them.'

'I see.'

'Then you've got the local gangs. When I first started here, a lot of the Hispanic kids in the South Bronx were in the Latin Kings, but they're not as strong as they used to be. The police arrested most of their leaders a while back, but I guess they're still around. Their main guy was sentenced to two hundred and fifty years in jail for murder, it was some sort of record, and he gets to spend the first forty-five years in solitary.'

Joseph let out a whistle at the prospect of forty-five years in solitary confinement, 'They were sure out to get him.'

'I guess they were.' She was stirring her coffee but her eyes never left his. 'The Dominicans have their own gang, the Trinitarios, and then there is the D.O.D..'

'The D.O.D.?'

'Stands for "Do Or Die" but they aren't so much a gang as a crew, or so I'm told.'

'What's the difference?'

She shrugged. 'I don't know, it's just what the kids say. They will tell you stuff sometimes. I think they view it as educating me for a change. The ones who aren't in gangs like to explain it all to me so I know how tough their lives are. I guess they are like "how can I possibly do my homework when the Bloods are standing on my corner?"'

'Yeah, that's probably it. Are there any other gangs or is that everybody?'

'Let's see, there's MS13 and Six Wild. Then there's the D.D.P., which means "Dominicans Don't Play" and a whole heap of others.

I once heard there are an estimated 15,000 gang members in New York alone and they say it is nowhere near as bad now as it used to be in the eighties and nineties.'

'And these tags they spray everywhere? Marking their territory?'

'Yep, either that or sending some other message to rival gangs, like when they paint over another gang's tags or spray a line through the name of a gang member, which means they are going to get him.'

Joseph took a sip of his coffee. When he spoke he tried to sound unconcerned, 'I saw a tag once in my neighbourhood. It had two initials on it – CK. Know what that means?'

Brigitte nodded, 'That would be Crips' Killers.'

'Right,' he said, trying to figure out how concerned he should be about the message sprayed on Eddie's door. 'There was another symbol right next to it, an inverted arrow.' He made a pointing gesture towards the floor.

'Mmm,' she said thoughtfully. 'Well, you know what that means?'

'No,' he admitted and she copied his gesture then aped the gangsta style of talking, putting on a deep voice and rolling her head about like she had an attitude.

'It means somebody's "going down".'

Brigitte continued to talk about gangs and their tags and the problems the school had with them. Joseph tried hard to listen to her without distraction but it wasn't easy. His good friend Eddie had been sent a clear message; the tag on his door was a death threat. The old man was in way too deep, far more so than he had admitted to Joseph and now it was hard to see how he could be protected. Joseph had to work for his living and was in his cab more often than not. He couldn't be with Eddie twenty-four-seven, even if the old man permitted it, which he wouldn't. Brigitte was still talking about her school and the measures the Principal was promising to take to make it safe for staff and pupils. Joseph was not really listening. Then he suddenly stopped her. 'What did you just say?'

'I said, I guess we'll hear all about it tomorrow at the parents' meeting. Everyone will be there staff, parents and police. You got the letter, right?'

'Yeah, sure, it's tomorrow night, right?' he asked absent-mindedly.

'What's wrong?' she asked, because he was already climbing to his feet, pulling small bills from his pocket to pay for the coffee and tip.

'Nothing. I've just got to get back that's all. Like I said I've got to see Eddie.'

Joseph banged a little too hard and a little too long on Eddie's freshly painted door. It would need another coat, for you could still make out the faint, red letters, CK, followed by the inverted arrow through the layer of white paint the old man had applied.

Eddie wasn't the quickest on his feet these days, but he would normally have answered his door by now. Joseph knocked again, knowing Eddie wouldn't have gone anywhere without telling him, but no reply came.

This wasn't like Eddie and Joseph began to fear for his friend. He knocked again and again, banging his fist harder and harder against the old man's door but all he got in return was silence.

8

Joseph had his cell phone in his hand and was dialling the emergency number when a harsh voice inside the apartment finally called, 'Yeah, yeah, I'm coming.' The door was opened cautiously, like the retired cop was braced for trouble. 'Oh, it's you,' he said but he resisted the temptation for a wisecrack when he saw the look on Joseph's face.

'What the hell was wrong? I've been banging on your door. Were you both asleep in there?'

'We had the ball game on. I didn't hear you,' growled Eddie. The TV was indeed at a deafening volume. Eddie obviously liked to feel he was actually at the game judging by the noise of the crowd. Joseph wondered if the old man's neighbours minded living next to Yankee Stadium.

'I need to speak to Yomi,' he explained. 'Right away.'

'Sure,' said Eddie. 'He's right here.' He called over his shoulder, 'Yomi, it's your pop. Hurry up now.'

'Thanks, Eddie,' said Joseph.

'No problem,' he said. Yomi was off the sofa and slowly pulling on his jacket, so Eddie used the interlude. 'Listen, Joseph, I think they're back.'

'Who is?'

'Those damn kids, using the lockup to store their stolen shit.'

'Right, well,' Joseph shrugged. This didn't seem like something he could become involved with and right now what he really needed was a moment alone with his son, 'what do you think we can do about it?'

'Well, we could check it out, the two of us this time, like you said,' Joseph frowned. Had he really said that? Had his lecture to the old man about the danger of acting on his own been somehow lost in translation? Still, Eddie did seem to feel strongly about this intrusion of the gangs onto their project. 'All right, but not now, okay?'

'Sure,' and the old man suggested they go down there a couple of days later. Joseph agreed he would set aside the time to take a look at the lockups. Between them they could evaluate what was going on down there and what, if anything, could be done about it. 'Are you okay, Joseph?' asked Eddie.

'I will be.'

Realising something was wrong, Eddie said, 'I won't stop by tonight, leave you guys to talk.'

Joseph just nodded his thanks then he glared at the boy as he emerged.

'What?' asked Yomi.

His father didn't answer. Instead he jerked his head in the direction of the staircase and walked silently behind his son all the way along the corridor and up the stairs until they reached their apartment. Joseph opened the door and nodded at the armchair. 'Sit,' he said.

'I ain't no dog,' answered Yomi, but he sat down anyway.

'Shut up,' said Joseph quietly, startling his son.

'What's wrong now?'

'Why didn't you tell me about the parents' meeting?'

'Oh,' said Yomi. 'How'd you find out about that?'

'Never mind how I found out, I found out, that's all that need concern you. Why didn't I find out about it from you?'

'I forgot.'

'Don't lie to me, Yomi.'

Now Yomi had adopted the sullen sulk approach, arms folded across his chest, mouth sealed, eyes staring off out of the window of their apartment as if he was gazing at a distant horizon.

'Okay then,' said Joseph. 'Let's assume you don't want to go because you've been carrying a knife and you are worried someone's going to mention it to the police while we are there. Can we assume that?'

Yomi shrugged. 'You're the detective.'

'Right! That's it!' Joseph rarely shouted

and his raised voice made his son start. 'I've had just about enough of this. I am sick and tired of your attitude, your backchat and your wise-assed comments. Son, I should have torn into you when I caught you with that knife but no, I was wrong. I cut you a lot of slack when you gave me that speech about the horrible apartment you live in, the crummy school you've got to go to and the fact you are so ashamed 'cos your daddy's just a cab driver, well that's all a crock and you know it. You are old enough to know better and, whatever your age, carrying a knife is the dumbest thing you've ever done. Only thing that guarantees is someone is going to get hurt. Probably you.' Joseph had his son's full attention now. 'I'm sorry things didn't work out the way I planned when Mom died and I brought you over here, but life is like that sometimes. I drive a cab and I see a lot of bad people every day but do you see me carrying a knife or a gun? No. We haven't got enough money but do you see me on the street corner selling drugs to make more? No. Instead, I work. Why? Because it's the right thing to do. I know you know the right thing to do, Yomi, so start doing it, as of now. You and I are going to that meeting tomorrow night and we are

110

going to listen to the police, the principal and anyone else that wants to shoot their mouth off there, no matter how uncomfortable it makes us feel. You got me?'

Yomi nodded like he suddenly realised just how far over the mark he had stepped. 'Now go to bed,' he told the boy, and Yomi went without a word. When he had gone Joseph sighed and slumped into the old armchair. Somewhere down below, off into the distance, police sirens were blaring.

The school hall was packed. All the teachers were there, each one standing like a sentry at the end of a row of chairs. On the stage in front of the lectern was a giant photograph of Hernando Lopez. It looked like the kind of thing you found in a school yearbook and it had been blown up so large the image had become a little blurred. Flowers had been placed on top of the hastily framed portrait.

The parents and their children packed into the hall and gradually filled the chairs that were set out in front of the stage. Joseph noticed McCavity, dressed in one of her dark, power suits, walking slowly up and down at the side of the room, surveying the scene before her as if she might be able to spot guilt written across the young faces in the crowd. Is she looking for another suspect? Had Jermaine admitted to having an accomplice, or had he confessed to taking the knife from Yomi?

The audience did not have to wait long for the opening address. Principal Decker walked out from the wings and stood stiffly in front of the lectern, right behind the portrait of the late Hernando Lopez. The principal slowly removed his glasses from a jacket pocket and put them on, using the manoeuvre to delay his speech long enough to bring the audience in front of him to a quiet. When he began to speak, his voice was deep and loud enough to reach the back of the room. Years of practice in front of a younger audience made public speaking easy for him. He gave a short speech of welcome, which turned into a eulogy for Hernando Lopez, 'a teacher who was greatly loved and respected by both pupils and colleagues alike, a man whose life has been cut cruelly short in its prime by the cowardly hand of a murderer'. He then led the whole audience in a recital of the Lord's prayer followed by a minute of personal, silent prayer for their dear departed teacher. This moment of tranquillity was suddenly shattered when an outer door slammed shut somewhere at the front of the building.

Two sets of parents then entered the hall sheepishly, shushing their offspring when they realised they had ruined the solemn moment. There was an uncomfortable interlude as people were forced to move along the aisles to admit the latecomers.

Decker surveyed these new arrivals as if they'd just pissed all over Hernando Lopez's grave, but he managed to keep his composure long enough to conclude the address. 'Now I would like to welcome our friends from the New York Police Department and would ask you all to do everything in your power to assist them in catching the killer of our dearly loved colleague. All of us owe it to the memory of Hernando Lopez to give our total commitment and support in finding his killer, nothing more, nothing less.' This indicated to Joseph that the cops may have arrested Jermaine Letts to assist with their enquiries but they had insufficient evidence to charge him for murder. It meant no confession had been forthcoming, so all options remained open. 'I will now hand you over to Assistant Chief McCavity of the 41st Precinct.' He held out an arm and McCavity began her ascent onto the stage. She was greeted by an eerie silence, which was to be expected. The usual welcoming applause for a visiting dignitary was entirely inappropriate under the circumstances. McCavity took to the stage with the practised ease of the career politician. Right now she was where she always liked to be, thought Joseph, in the centre of attention.

'Thank you for welcoming me to your community,' she began, as if anyone there had even known she was coming, 'and allowing me to speak with you here tonight.' She was adopting the posture of the humble public servant. 'I am only sorry that the occasion is marked by such a far-reaching tragedy as this one. I am here to assure you that we in the NYPD are doing everything possible to maintain the safety of you, your children, and their dedicated teachers. We are devoting every available resource towards solving this heinous crime, a crime that in many ways was directed against us all.'

Somewhere from the back of the hall there was a faintly audible, exasperated muttering of the word 'Jesus'. Joseph got the impression that this was not uttered by a religious man.

McCavity continued unperturbed. 'I am also here tonight to plead for your help in catching the cold-blooded killer of your much-loved educator Hernando Lopez.' Lopez had been a teacher when he was alive, pondered Joseph. Now that he was dead, they had turned him into an educator.

'You can help us in one very simple way. We are asking you all to grant your permission tonight for us to finger print your children in order to rule them out of our investigation and narrow the search for this callous killer.' She was doing pretty good until that point, thought Joseph, but now he realised she had completely underestimated her audience. He was heartened to hear the volatility of the reaction. The last thing he wanted was Yomi to have to stand in line with the other kids, waiting to get his fingerprints taken, knowing they were already on the murder weapon. There was an immediate ramping up of volume, which sounded like a collective sharp intake of breath, and then the comments began, hurled at McCavity like accusations.

'You wanna do what?'

This was followed by 'no way you goin' fingerprint my little gal'.

Then there was the inevitable cry of 'get the fuck out of here!'

After that the comments became indecipherable and all of them melded into one. McCavity was forced to repeatedly appeal for calm.

In the end, Principal Decker had to come back onto the stage to plead with everyone. 'Please! Please! Let the assistant chief speak. Please, let's have some order here and some respect for our fallen colleague.'

There was a temporary lull, and McCavity attempted to explain her request. She held up a placatory hand. 'I understand feelings are running high...'

Someone shouted, 'Damn right they are!'

'That's only natural, but we are not implying that your children are criminals.' She tried a little false laugh to underline the absurdity of such an idea. 'This is merely to assist us in finding a killer. That's what we should most concern ourselves with here.'

A well-dressed, black lady with an educated voice stood up and said clearly, 'What I am most concerned with is the infringement of my son's civil liberties.'

There were loud cries of support and applause and McCavity looked a little shocked by the reaction she had provoked. 'Please, this is America. I can assure you nobody is at risk of having their liberties infringed in any way.'

'Tell that to those guys down at Camp X-Ray,' shouted someone from the middle of the room, to a mixed reaction.

Some people shouted 'yeah' and 'that's right', others seemed to have decided that civil liberties were for citizens of the South Bronx only and not applicable to foreigners suspected of terrorist offences.

'No, really,' continued McCavity, as if she considered that to be an entirely irrelevant comparison. 'We have a number of sets of prints on or around the murder scene and we merely want to narrow our search for possible suspects.'

Joseph had every reason to hope her plea would fall on deaf ears and he was pleased to see another parent stand up, an Italian-American lady, who spoke calmly. 'Firstly, you have a number of fingerprints on or around the murder scene because it happens to be a classroom.' There were loud whoops of support at this abrupt debunking of the police methodology. 'And secondly I would like to ask what you intend to do if you match my daughter's fingerprints to one of the desks in that room. Does that rule her out or make her a suspect.'

More cries of 'yeah!' from the audience

'Look, we have to do everything we can to ensure that this killer is brought to justice...' McCavity began.

'Excuse me,' interrupted the first black

woman who had spoken, 'would you stop acting like a god dammed politician and just answer her question?'

Huge uproar now, massed support, McCavity was losing the argument big style. The detective was being assailed on all sides by outraged parents, who were climbing to their feet to compete with one another, so they could contribute to the debate. Joseph was willing to bet McCavity had already realised she had no chance of getting her fingerprinting idea through now.

The cacophony was so loud it was impossible to make out individual arguments until someone stood up right at the back of the room and a deep male voice boomed, 'What you want to fingerprint everybody for anyhow, you got the damn killer, everybody knows it!'

More uproar and some strong agreement from a lot of angry people.

McCavity shouted back, 'Yes, we have a suspect in custody at the moment and we hope to be able to bring charges against that person, who I cannot name at this juncture, but that does not necessarily mean...'

She was drowned out again and looked as if she was about to give up any attempt at addressing the room. Then a strange thing happened. The audience suddenly fell silent, swiftly and without complaint. It was like one of those old black-and-white westerns they used to show on TV on Saturday mornings in Lagos, where the whole saloon falls silent because the gunslinger with the black hat just walked in and stared everybody down.

When Joseph looked round at what had caused this sudden compliance, he saw an emaciated, grim-faced black lady standing at the back of the room, with a young teenager, who looked like she could be her daughter, at her side. This middle-aged woman had tired, sunken eyes and everything about her gaunt appearance made it look as if she had been beaten down by life but there was a look of steely resolve about her today. That look said 'don't mess with me' and she was staring straight up at McCavity, her face like thunder.

A young voice near Joseph whispered, 'That's Jermaine Letts' mom.'

The assistant chief was confused by the silence that accompanied Mrs Letts' entrance. It seemed everyone was keen to hear what she had to say about her murdering son. 'Would you like to say something?' she asked, looking a little flustered.

'I'm here tonight to say one thing to you

all and one thing only, so listen up.' Her voice was frail and husky, a smoker's growl, and her eyes moved from face to face in the audience, she was staring them all down, the whole room one person at a time. 'My son Jermaine ain't no altar boy, I'm not denying it, but he ain't no killer, neither. Damn fool police are saying he done stabbed his teacher, the very idea.' She snorted her derision and even McCavity seemed taken aback, 'Jermaine liked that teacher, Mr Lopez, and he is telling the truth. He admits the knife that killed the teacher was the one he had taken off him but he didn't stab the poor man. He's innocent, you hear?'

At that moment, Principal Decker must have decided he'd heard enough. His meeting had been hijacked by a succession of aggrieved parents and now they were all being talked down to by the mother of a murder suspect. He cleared his throat and said, 'Mrs Letts, we have all heard the story that your son had a knife taken off him in class by Mr Lopez but if that was the case your boy would have been instantly expelled. We have a very clear policy of zero tolerance on knife crime. If Mr Lopez had found a knife on Jermaine, he would have walked him straight down to my office, the police would have been called and your son would have been suspended pending full, permanent exclusion. That's the policy.'

Mrs Letts was unimpressed. 'So you got a policy, huh, principal? I'm happy for you. Bet you got a whole lot of policies about a whole heap of things, don't mean anyone listens to you for a damn minute. You ever thought that teacher might not be so dumb as to expel someone for carrying a knife in a neighbourhood where it's harder to find someone who don't carry a knife? Ever think of that? Now if the police here get off their fat asses and ask around, they'll find a whole room full of people that saw my son get a knife taken off him by that teacher. And you didn't hear a damn thing about it at the time. Was that in your god dammed policy? No, it weren't. So it seems to me you really ain't in control of this place at all Mr Principal.'

She could not have chosen a better way to silence Decker. His mouth gaped as if he was about to try and rebuff the claims of this tiny woman, but he did not seem able to accept the concept of a lack of total control over Antoinette Irving and the notion stopped him in his tracks. Before he could say anything, she carried on. 'Jermaine goin' be proved innocent, you'll see it and when all this is over...' She pointed a bony finger at Decker. 'I hope the principal over here goin' throw another big public meeting so you can all apologise to him in person. That's all I got to say,' and she turned with some dignity for such a rough-looking woman and walked out of the building.

Her daughter lingered for a moment, surveyed the room scornfully and said, 'We done with you,' before walking unhurriedly after her mother, hips swaying from side to side in a swaggering fuck-you roll.

9

Joseph knocked on the office door and a moment later a formal voice filled with self-importance answered, 'Enter.'

Principal Decker looked as if he had yet to sufficiently recover from the ordeal of the evening. Joseph could understand why. His carefully thought-out tribute to Mr Lopez and his heart-felt appeal for assistance for the fine officers of the New York Police Department had all fallen on deaf ears. The way he would view it, his public meeting had become little more than a slanging match between an ill-disciplined rabble of parents and a senior police officer and, to cap it all, a murder suspect's mom had upstaged everybody, poured scorn on his proceedings then flounced out of the room like a diva, leaving little more than chaos and uproar behind her as she went. In any event, the meeting had broken up in an unstructured manner soon after the departure of Mrs Letts.

'Can I help you, Mr Soyinka?' asked Principal Decker in a tone that made it clear he would rather do anything but. He then added, 'I really am incredibly busy right now.'

'I would appreciate a moment of your time. I'd like to talk to you.'

'What about?'

'The murder of Mr Lopez.'

'I see,' he said primly. 'Do you have some information you wish me to relay to the police?'

'No,' and I wouldn't come to you with it if I did, thought Joseph.

'Then I'm not sure how I can help.' He still had not admitted Joseph to his room.

'I have a question about the locked classroom. I was wondering how many people had access to the keys for Mr Lopez's door?'

'I'm sorry?' Principal Decker had a look

on his face that showed he was dumbfounded by the question. 'Do you have some form of familial link to Mr Lopez that I am perhaps unaware of?'

'No.'

'Or perhaps you are related to Jermaine Letts in some way?'

'No.'

'Then since you have already admitted you can provide no new information to the police I cannot possibly see what business it is of yours to be asking such questions.'

'I find it interesting you say it's none of my business when a while ago, during your eulogy, you said "all of us owe it to the memory of Hernando Lopez to give our total commitment and support in finding his killer, nothing more, nothing less". Did I get that right? That was what you said wasn't it? Or did you just not really mean it?'

The principal sighed wearily, which meant he was pretending to be ground down by Joseph's tenacity and was perhaps prepared to indulge him this one time. It was either that or he would have to admit the obvious contradiction in his words. Decker opened the door of his office wide to allow Joseph to come in. 'You may as well sit down,' he said begrudgingly. 'Now what is your point, Mr Soyinka?'

'My point is that here was a bright and intelligent man who was stabbed in the corridor of the school and was left severely injured, supposedly by a young boy. Instead of heading for the nearest phone and dialling 911, he holes up in his classroom, locks himself in and bleeds to death.'

Decker was baffled. 'Well, he was locking himself inside the room to escape his assailant, surely.'

'That's the bit I don't buy; that a fourteen-year-old boy would calmly wait outside the classroom door and watch while his teacher slowly bled to death in front of him, without worrying that someone else might walk by and catch him red handed. Remember the knife was found in the classroom near Lopez's body, so he couldn't have been scared he'd be stabbed with it again.'

'Excuse me, but is this some form of bizarre hobby of yours, interfering in police investigations like some latter-day Sherlock Holmes? I mean, it's not the first time you have done this, is it? I was there when Detective McCavity renewed your acquaintance. Don't you think the professional detectives of the NYPD might have a slightly better understanding of the facts of this case than you? What is it that validates your opinion exactly?'

Joseph didn't like to admit to his past, but he realised the principal had left him with little option. 'Twenty years as a senior detective, investigating robberies and homicides, plus the letter of commendation I received from Assistant Chief McCavity the last time I "interfered" in her investigation. I think that validates my opinion, don't you?' He could tell by Decker's face that this was a shock to him. 'What I'm beginning to wonder is why you seem so reluctant to answer my question when all I'm trying to do is help.'

'I'm not reluctant to answer your question,' declared a flustered Decker and, when Joseph stayed silent, he realised he'd painted himself into a corner. 'There are only three sets of keys for that classroom or any other classroom, come to mention it. One is mine and one set is the janitor's, the third is a master set but it stays in the school safe at all times in case of an emergency. No one has access to that set except me. The janitor's keys supposedly stay with your friend Ardo at all times. He has sworn as much to the police and myself, for what that's worth.'

'Only three sets, no spares left lying around that could be picked up?'

'Just the three sets, Mr Soyinka, like I said.' Decker was trying to recover his composure. 'And since you are the detective, I should add that I have a cast-iron alibi for the night of the murder. I was having dinner with my wife in a busy restaurant. I am sure the waiter at Fiorentino's will remember me.' I'm sure he will, thought Joseph. 'Incidentally, which police force did you say you were with?'

'I didn't. It was the NPF in Lagos. The Nigerian Police Force.'

'Oh,' said Decker, as if Joseph had told him he was in the army then suddenly admitted it was actually the Salvation Army.

'I realise you find this hard to believe Principal Decker, but it wasn't all like the Number One Ladies' Detective agency. We were professional police officers, we had our fair share of gangsters, murderers and low-lifes to contend with, and we did bring many of them to justice.'

'I'm sure you did, Mr Soyinka, really I am.' The man spoke like he was a character in a Jane Austen novel, thought Joseph. Bet he wished he was born English, so that priggishness would sound even more authentic. 'But I still cannot see what you're getting at with this business of the keys.'

'It's very simple really,' explained Joseph. 'I'm saying I don't believe Hernando Lopez locked himself in the classroom. I'm saying the murderer locked him in there and left him to bleed to death.'

It was as well Principal Decker was already sitting down, for this disclosure clearly rocked him. 'Are you serious?'

'Perfectly.'

'You're saying a child from this school is capable of such cold-hearted...'

'I didn't say anything about a child,' said Joseph quietly. 'The police have yet to prove it was a child. I'm simply stating that in my view whoever did this locked Lopez in his room and quite possibly watched him die.'

Confronted with the enormity of this notion, Decker seemed to lose all his fight and hostility. Letting down his guard for a moment he said, 'When the meeting broke up tonight, Assistant Chief McCavity admitted to me privately that the police are going to have to let Jermaine Letts go.'

It clearly caused Decker discomfort to concede this. 'His prints are on the knife but they would be, it was in his possession when Mr Lopez took it off him earlier in the day. I'm afraid, much as it pains me to admit it, that Mrs Letts was correct. A number of witnesses can back that up.'

'So Lopez took a knife off the boy but didn't report him?'

'It seems Mr Lopez decided to ignore our rigid policy on knife carrying,' he admitted. 'It may even have cost him his life. After all, the knife would not have still been on his person if he had come to me with it. I would have locked it in the safe out of harm's way.'

'However there is nothing except the fingerprints to link Jermaine Letts to this terrible crime and he apparently has no discernible motive. They also tell me his prints are not clean edged, which means they were under the blood on the knife.'

Joseph had got far more out of his interview with Principal Decker than he could have hoped for. 'Thank you, Principal,' he said and he left Decker to ponder the wreckage of his evening.

As Joseph pulled the cab out of the gates of Antoinette Irving, armed with this significant new information on the Lopez case, he felt a little easier. Then he spotted Yomi and several of his friends some way up the street. They were walking together in that slow and aimless teenage manner, like they were going no place and in no particular hurry to get to it. Joseph had assumed Yomi would welcome a lift home, as it was another bitterly cold night, so he sounded the horn of the Crown Victoria but there was no reaction from his son. When he drew closer, he waved, but the boy kept his head down then seemed to deliberately look away. As he drove past, Joseph heard one of the other boys call, 'Hey, Yomi, it's your old man!' It was said with an accompanying laugh, in a mocking manner, like his father was a circus clown or polished shoes for a living. Joseph had all the proof he needed. His son was clearly ashamed of him.

Fine, thought Joseph, let him walk home with his friends, let's see how he enjoys it in this weather. He'll be freezing by the time he gets back to the project. Joseph told himself that this was the least of his worries, even though it hurt him to be snubbed by his son like that. He had begun that evening thinking Yomi was going to be dragged into a police investigation. For now, he was just glad McCavity's grand fingerprinting scheme had been shot down in flames by the good citizens of the South Bronx and his boy was no longer in the frame for a murder.

Usually, when Joseph dropped Yomi at school

130

in the morning, he turned the cab right around and went looking for some early money outside the few hotels in the area that were smart enough to accommodate businessmen. These days there was always a property deal or a development meeting, involving suited government officials and venture capitalists with more money than brains. Some of them would be looking to get to the airport right after their power breakfast and every now and then he could pick-up a juicy fare to La Guardia. Today was going to be different however. Joseph dropped his son and waited till Yomi had disappeared into the building, then he drove across the school car park into a far corner that was shielded from view by a row of birch trees and he parked up. Then he went looking for Ardo.

Technically he could have been accused of trespassing by a principal who was likely to be in a less than forgiving mood following their last exchange. However, he hadn't actually entered the school as such. Instead, he skirted round the side of the building looking for the janitor. Principal Decker was aware of their friendship so, if challenged, Joseph could say he was just dropping by to invite Ardo for a game of chess after school.

Joseph headed for the block that housed the

school's ancient, creaking boiler, its garbage compactor and paper-shredding machines. Here was the small enclave that Ardo Piloyan called his own. Joseph found the door to the block unlocked and he peered inside, eyes blinking to adjust to the gloom, his senses disoriented by the loud insistent whir from the boiler and the grating noise of the compactor that was being used to destroy something.

'Ardo?' he called. 'That you?'

When he received no answer, he called again, louder this time but the response was the same. Strange. Joseph decided to venture inside. The room was large and dark and littered with hazards for a tall man like Joseph who had stepped into it from a bright, hazy but bitterly cold morning. He almost stumbled down a couple of small steps and bumped his head on an overhanging pipe that had thankfully been lagged with insulation padding. The air was dry and riddled with dust flecks that had been kicked up by the vibration of heavy machinery. Joseph walked along a small corridor that opened out into a large L-shaped room.

'Ardo,' he called once more, concern in his voice this time. There was still no reply and Joseph realised the noise of the room was louder than normal. The compactor seemed to be stuck on its loudest setting, like it had been ground to a halt by whatever was wedged inside it. There was no sign of his friend.

Joseph began to experience a bad feeling, an instinct that things were not as they were meant to be, which was exacerbated by the grating off-kilter sound coming from the compactor. There was something big in there, something that had clogged up the machinery, something that shouldn't have been put into an industrial-sized compactor. Joseph swallowed hard then walked slowly and tentatively right up to the creaking contraption. He reached the edge and was forced to stand on tiptoe to peer over it. Then he glanced down into the guts of the machine. He barely dared to look inside.

'Holy Christ!' someone shouted from behind him. Joseph span round to see Ardo standing there, a look of bemusement on his face. 'What have you done?' cried the Janitor.

'I haven't done anything,' blurted Joseph. 'I came looking for you. It was making that damned racket when I arrived. I thought you'd fallen in.' Thought you'd been pushed in, more like, by a bloodthirsty street gang.

It sounded ridiculous now, with Ardo standing there in front of him, entirely unharmed. What outlandish theory had Joseph concocted in his overwrought mind? Ardo had been shoved into the compactor by the junior high school's Marine-Corps-trained football coach during a bout of post-traumatic stress, perhaps? Maybe a disgruntled Principal Decker had snapped, following his publicly humiliating parents' meeting and taken it out on the little Armenian or, better still, Brigitte De Moyne had gone postal, killing all of her colleagues with the gun Joseph had taught her to use, then feeding them to the compactor one by one. Joseph didn't know what moment of madness had compelled him to peer inside the machine. He was just relieved to see Ardo standing there looking alarmed and not a little pissed off at his uninvited presence in the boiler room.

The little Armenian strode past Joseph and banged the big, red off switch with the palm of his hand. The machine juddered once in protest, as if breathing its last, then it quietly expired, instantly bringing an ear-ringing silence to the room.

'God damn that fucking piece of shitty American engineering,' proclaimed Ardo.

'You know where it was made? Iowa. Who the fuck you know ever been to Iowa?' And with that profound pronouncement behind him he demanded, 'You want coffee or what?'

The old metal kettle was filled with water, placed on a tiny stove and slowly coaxed to the boil. Joseph looked around Ardo's private corner of the stockroom and noticed there were a couple of power points but it was clear Ardo had an old-fashioned attitude towards kettles. This one had no flex and there was even a whistle on the top to let you know when the water had finished boiling. The old Armenian must have viewed electric white goods in the same suspicious manner that Joseph saw the i-Pod, as a clever but complicated modern device he had no discernible need for.

Ardo laughed. 'You really think I was in there?' He nodded at the broken compactor as he handed Joseph his coffee.

'Of course not.' He accepted the mug gratefully, wrapping his hands round its heat, for no matter how near he sat to the propane heater he couldn't seem to remove the chill from his bones. The room was too big and poorly insulated to be entirely warmed by the hulking old boiler in winter time, but Ardo must have grown used to its drafts for he did not seem at all uncomfortable down here. There were few home comforts in his room, save for a cork noticeboard that contained postcards from friends and relatives in Europe and a couple of faded pictures of his grown-up children and grandchildren.

'Nice of you to come see me, Joseph.'

'It's always good to see you, Ardo, I enjoy your company and our little games.'

Ardo laughed. 'Want me to go get the board?' It seemed that was all the excuse he needed to play hooky from his work for a while.

Joseph shook his head. 'I'll be honest with you. Today I'm here for a different reason.'

'Not chess? No? What is it, my friend?' said the janitor earnestly. 'You need help from Ardo? Anything, you just name it.'

Joseph found he was touched by Ardo's instant willingness to lend him a hand. 'No, nothing like that. I'm afraid it's about the Hernando Lopez killing,' he admitted and went on to explain his theory about the keys and his increasing suspicion that the teacher had been locked in his classroom and left there to die.

Ardo seemed a little taken aback by this.

136

'The police, they ask me, come on, Ardo, they say, who else had a key? Who you lend it to? And I tell them, nobody. Ardo gives his key to nobody. But that doesn't stop them with their questions. One of them even asked me if I gave my keys to the young boy, Jermaine, and then he asked me what I got the boy to do to earn those keys. Can you imagine? I told him to shut his filthy mouth. I ask him what kind of dirty, disgusting mind think up a question like that, and him a police officer? I told him he should be ashamed to think like that. He just laughed at me, Joseph, he laughed.'

Ardo went on to give Joseph a lengthy explanation about the sanctity of his keys, the fact that he would never let them out of his sight, let alone dream of giving or lending them to anyone else. Ardo explained that he was trusted by the school and the state of New York with those keys, they were his responsibility and he took that responsibility very seriously. Ardo went on at such length that Joseph began to regret asking him such an emotive question. Then he suddenly noticed something.

'Ardo, you always wear those keys on your belt right?'

'Sure.'

'So, where are they now?'

'Now,' Ardo blinked quickly and looked a little embarrassed. 'You mean right now?'

'Yes, I mean right now.'

'Well, I don't wear them every second of the day, Joseph, got to take them off some time, like when I go to the crapper maybe.'

'That where you just been?'

'What?' he said incredulously. 'I can't believe you ask me that. You want to know if I just been for a shit. No, I clean windows. Every week I got to clean windows, always with the windows, there are so many so I am always cleaning them, two, sometimes three times a week. See the way I do it is I clean some, not all of them but some each time. That way I get round them all and Decker can't find an excuse to fire my ass. The damned man don't like me Joseph. I don't think he likes anybody who weren't born here.'

'And you don't wear your keys when you clean the windows?'

'You want me to break my neck on the god dammed ladder? No, I don't wear my keys when I clean the windows, Joseph. I am up ladder. If keys get caught in ladder they make me fall and I perkush...' and he made a sound like something falling onto the hard ground from a great height, bringing the flat of his palm down swiftly against his knee to illustrate this grim fate.

'I understand,' said Joseph and he nodded vigorously to calm his friend down. 'So, where are the keys right now, Ardo?'

10

Joseph was headed for Merve Williams' hardware store, one hand resting on the steering wheel of the cab, coaxing it through the traffic, the other absent-mindedly toying with the heavy clump of keys in his lap. The ones Ardo never let out of his sight. The ones Ardo had just given him.

Ardo had agreed to lend him the keys for two reasons. 'I only do this because it is you, Joseph,' he assured his friend. 'Only you I trust this much, like a brother, to borrow my keys and bring them safe back to me after lunch, like you promise, okay.' He was nervous, as well he might be. The other reason for his generous agreement to permit Joseph the set of keys had remained unspoken between them. It was the obvious embarrassment in Ardo's eyes when he showed Joseph the nail in the noticeboard that was pinned to the wall in the corner of his unlocked room. This he had admitted was where he left his keys when he was up the ladder, covering the school windows in soapsuds. Joseph was fairly certain that when Ardo had sworn to the police, on his family's honour and his children's lives, that he never leant his keys to anyone else, he had unwittingly neglected to mention the two maybe three times a week he hung them on a nail in an unlocked boiler room while he was washing windows. It was Ardo's combination of embarrassment and fear that had prompted Joseph to request the loan of his keys for just an hour or two. Reluctantly, the Armenian had complied.

Now that he had proven one important thing; that other people could get hold of the supposedly well-guarded keys while Ardo was up a ladder, Joseph was about to try and prove another; that he could get a copy of those same keys made in the time it took Ardo to wipe down another set of windows.

Merve Williams' hardware store was an exception for a small business in that corner of the South Bronx. It was thriving. Merve might not be a millionaire but his hard-earned reputation, keen eye for a bargain and attention to detail had ensured him a loyal enough clientele to keep the ever-present spectre of Wal-Mart from his door. While other businesses closed down around him, robbed of a level playing field by the Starbucks and K-Mart buy 'em-cheap, pile-'em-high and discount-'em-low approach, he had quietly thrived. He'd even taken on the lease of the retail lot next door when it inevitably fell vacant. In short, he had a thrifty, seemingly recession-proof business because in his own simple words, 'people always gonna need nails'.

Merve was a big, powerful man and he probably needed to be round here. There was always someone in the South Bronx only too ready to hit you for the takings or jack a few power drills out from under you when your back was turned. Power tools were high up on the popularity lists of petty criminals along with portable, electrical goods. They were easy to transport, desirable to own but expensive if you had to pay the full retail price. It was a simple question of supply and demand and their desirability made them easier to fence. Merve had obviously borne that in mind when he set up his business. There were CCTV cameras everywhere, both outside of the store and in, with warning signs about a patrolling security service provided by a firm with a tough-sounding name.

Merve was standing behind the counter in that grim, unsmiling, masculine way they always did in those hardware stores, none of that saccharin-sweet have-a-nice-day attitude here. Merve's customers just wanted to get to the point, buy their power tools and lumber and get out of there.

'Merve, how you doing?'

'Getting by,' answered Merve grimly, as if life was one long struggle he was just about on top of.

'How are the girls?'

'Good,' he said it quickly, almost defensively. 'They're always a worry though, girls. My boy don't give me no trouble but the girls? I got grey hair and bit-down nails from them. You've got a boy of course, so you wouldn't understand, but it's hard for girls round here. They got to be as tough as the boys these days.'

'Sure do,' agreed Joseph. He was wondering why Merve was giving him this little insight into the difficulties faced by young women in their area. Had Macy been up to

142

something she wouldn't want written about in her yearbook? 'Like you say, I got a boy and he's a good kid but he's trouble enough. I don't think I'd like to be sitting at home worrying about a girl.'

'I've learned worrying don't solve nothing and it don't change a thing. You've just got to let 'em work things out for themselves. It's like Macy, she was friends with that Letts girl, the one from the parent's evening,' and he gave Joseph a look that said all it needed to about the way he viewed young Miss Letts. Joseph remembered the tough-looking young girl with the hip rolling and the attitude. 'That worried me, I can tell you. She's trash. Whole family is no good, never has been, but Macy didn't want to listen to her old pop about a thing like that. Nothing I could say was going to stop them hanging round together. Might as well try and tell the rain to quit pouring, the good it would do. You know what happened? In the end they fell out over a boy or something, you know how girls can be. Can't say I was heart-broken when it happened though.'

Joseph recalled Macy Williams when she had put in an appearance down by the football field, flying by in her pick-up, waving like she owned the place and everyone in it. She looked tough enough to survive all right. He wondered how a quietly spoken, serious-minded, working man felt about his daughter's flamboyant appearance at the football practice. He doubted Merve Williams would approve.

'Your youngest is in Yomi's class, isn't she?'

'Laura? Yes, she is, says your boy's got all the smarts.'

Joseph laughed. 'Must get that from his mother.' He was trying to sound modest but was secretly proud of his son's academic prowess. 'Does Laura like school?'

'She did,' he said. 'She's a little upset about that teacher right now.'

'Who wouldn't be,' agreed Joseph.

'Yeah,' said Merve. 'Seems like he was a popular guy. I guess he must have had a way with the young ones, if you know what I mean. Anyway, Joseph, what can I do for you?'

'You still got that key-cutting booth?'

'Right out back. Kyle will see to you,' he turned round and hollered across the shop floor, 'Kyle!' A young guy with a face full of freckles and an unruly mop of ginger hair came running like Merve's word was the law. 'Mr Soyinka here needs some keys cutting.'

'Sure,' said Kyle and he led the way past racks piled high with timber and shelves filled with every tool a handyman could wish for as he ushered Joseph to the back of the store. There, in a dark little recess, was the key cutting machine. 'So, what you got?' asked Kyle.

Joseph held up the bunch of keys and the tacky, green Statue of Liberty key ring Ardo used and he handed them over to Kyle. The young man weighed them in his hand, as if that might make a difference to the price, then asked, 'We doing one of each?'

'I guess,' said Joseph. 'How much is that gonna be?'

'Let's see,' and he started counting the keys, mumbling the numbers out loud. When he'd finished he looked up as if he had suddenly remembered something. 'You got the card on you, right?'

'Excuse me?' Joseph asked it absent-mindedly as if he had not heard the boy.

'The ID card that goes with the master set. I can't cut any new keys without seeing the card first.'

'Oh, dang,' and Joseph put his hand to his head like that was all he needed right now. 'I don't believe it. I am such a dumb bunny. I forgot all about the card and left it behind,' he gave Kyle an imploring look. 'Say, there's no way you could just go ahead and cut them anyway and we'll say I'll bring the card in next time?'

'Oh, no, I'm sorry, sir.' Kyle looked shocked at the very notion. 'That right there'd be illegal.'

'I see,' said Joseph. 'No, you're right, it's my fault. I'll just come back another time. Thanks for your help.'

'That's what I'm here for,' said Kyle earnestly. 'Have a nice day.'

As Joseph drove the cab back to Antoinette Irving High School, he had to admit he was back to square one. He had proved it was possible to get access to the school keys when it was meant to be impossible but it was still far from clear how anybody could get a new set cut before returning them. Of course not every hardware store in New York was as straight as Merve's and not every key cutter as earnest and diligent as Kyle. There was no time to try anywhere else just now though. The keys had to go back to Ardo before he passed out from the stress of having them removed from his care. As he drove back to the school, Joseph glanced at his watch. Damn, he was running late. He now regretted being so cavalier in agreeing to accompany Eddie that afternoon on their foolish patrol of the neighbourhood. The stolen goods being cached in the lockups on their project were really not too high on his list of priorities right now. But Eddie was a good friend and, though he had a soft centre, his hard exterior could be instantly activated if he felt slighted or someone had failed to take him sufficiently seriously. It meant Joseph would have to move fast if Eddie wasn't going to be mightily pissed at his tardiness.

The knock on the front door of Eddie's apartment went unanswered, which meant the stubborn old guy had gone on ahead without him. Sure, Joseph was a little late but Eddie could have hung on for him before charging on down there like some lone vigilante. The lockups weren't going anywhere after all. Joseph sighed. He couldn't leave his friend to pursue a one-man war against the local gangs without any help, so he headed straight back down the staircase.

To get to the lockups, Joseph was forced to cross the children's play area, overlooked on all four sides by the towering apartment blocks of the Highbridge Project. It was set in a crumbling concrete base surrounded by a two-foot high fence made of metal hoops that might as well have not been there for all the purpose it served. It certainly wouldn't keep out anyone who shouldn't be there.

These days you rarely saw young kids playing here anymore. Instead, the whole space had been taken over by older teenagers. There were gang tags sprayed on the nearest wall, some of which looked suspiciously familiar. The crew that targeted Eddie's front door had obviously been busy, judging by the number of Crips' Killers tags decorating the nearby buildings. As he walked, his shoe crunched shards of glass from broken bottles into the concrete and he began to watch where he was treading in case there were syringes hidden under the litter that remained uncollected round these parts. Refuse crews were reluctant to work such a bad area and when they did they were none too thorough, fearing a stoning from the rooftops and balconies above them from bored kids with a sitting target down below. Joseph wondered if the playground had once been a nice spot, used by children, or if it had always been like it was today, a shit hole populated by gangs and junkies.

He reached the corner of the Highbridge

Project given over to the lockups and rounded the bend. That was when he saw Eddie and this time there was no cheery wave or jovial banter from the prone figure, nor did the old man attempt to raise himself from the ground. Eddie was lying flat on the cold, hard concrete. He was completely immobile, with his head lolled to one side, facing away from Joseph.

'Eddie,' he called as he ran towards the lifeless figure and squatted down next to him. 'Eddie, it's me, Joseph.'

The eyes were closed, the face pale and grey except for the scrapes and bruises that were already forming there. Joseph felt Eddie's neck for a pulse and was rewarded by the weakest of beats. It was then he noticed the matted blood on the side of Eddie's head that had been hidden from view when it was pressed against the ground. The old man could have banged his head as he fell but more likely this was the result of a heavy blow to the skull. Someone had sideswiped the old guy and left him there. Eddie looked in a bad way. Joseph thrust a hand into his jacket, pulled the cell phone from his pocket and frantically dialled 911.

11

Joseph had ridden in the back of the ambulance with Eddie all the way to the hospital. Now the old man was unconscious in a bed on one of the wards while his friend paced and fretted in a waiting room downstairs. Joseph was not feeling good about himself. He had been there hours and been afforded plenty of time to contemplate his role in all of this. He knew he had let his friend down, his guilt compounded by the fact that he was only too aware of the kind of man Eddie was. He could have laid even money that the old cop would have cursed Joseph for his lack of punctuality, taken it as a sign of disinterest on his friend's part and felt slighted, then gone down to investigate the lockups all by himself.

Whatever Eddie had found down there, it had only served to put him on the wrong end of a severe beating. Eddie was still a big man but the muscle he had been so proud of in his youth had softened with age and he was no longer all that mobile. The former tough guy would have been easy prey to a young and ruthless gang with a beef against an interfering ex-cop.

Pacing, Joseph was far from alone in the waiting room. By the time they had got Eddie into the hospital emergency department it was late afternoon and patients were coming in from all corners, victims of industrial accident, domestic abuse or any number of fights and mishaps caused by an afternoon's drinking. There were so many people there that relatively minor problems were being dealt with by a cursory examination and a seat in the waiting room alongside the relatives of the more severely afflicted. A girl who may or not have been a junkie was hugging herself in a corner while she sobbed and rocked back and forth, looking like she was about to go out of her mind with worry at the fate of a friend or lover. There was a large, stubble-faced guy dressed like a construction worker who was trying not to show too much concern at the big, blood-soaked bandage he was pressing against one eye. Somewhere through the double doors a small child was screaming for his mummy while the doctors tried to examine a broken bone. His anguished cries were enough to make anyone feel for the poor little guy.

Joseph tried to ignore the screams and the sobbing around him. Instead, he stared straight ahead at the double doors Eddie had been wheeled through, feeling like a failure. He was no good as a father, clearly hadn't been good enough to get into the NYPD and, to cap it all, he had now proven a dead loss as a friend. All he could do was wait and he did, for hours, while the poor old guy was in surgery, under the knife in a desperate bid to save his life. Joseph knew it didn't look good. He could tell by the grim-faced, no-nonsense way the ER team had spirited Eddie away on the gurney, moving as swiftly as the hospitals shiny floors would allow them. That had been hours ago. The light had long since gone and the numbers in the waiting room had diminished until there were but a few left around him. There were one or two able-bodied people and he wondered who they were waiting for, what road accident or mugging their loved ones were the victim of and their likely odds of survival. He thought about odds and statistics. If their loved ones survived, would that diminish Eddie's chances of pulling through. He knew that was nonsense. They would just as likely all make it or none of them would.

Finally, a harassed-looking young doctor

walked out through the door and called his surname, mispronouncing it as always.

Joseph had been waiting so long that he almost did not respond to his own name. 'Yes,' he replied dumbly, and the doctor came over and spoke to him in a discreet whisper.

'Your friend has a suspected fractured skull and severe concussion, a couple of broken ribs and a fracture of the right kneecap. That's the bad news. The good news is he is still with us and it's now just a question of waiting for him to wake up, so we can see what effect the blow to the head has had on him. That might be some time and your friend's age is obviously a factor that will hinder his recovery. My advice to you would be to go home now and get some rest. If you leave a number at the desk, someone will call you when we have more news.'

'Thank you, doctor,' said Joseph, and he climbed wearily to his feet. He left his number with the lady on the admittance desk and walked out into the cold night air to ponder Eddie's chances of recovery. He had taken quite a beating but he was a tough old guy, a fighter and it sounded like he had a fair chance of making it. Right now, after the shock he had received when he saw Eddie lying lifeless on the concrete, Joseph would settle for that.

Joseph returned to his apartment. He didn't bother to disturb Yomi, who would be tucked up on Marjorie's put-me-up sofa in her apartment by now. He had called the old lady to ask her if she would look after his son as soon as he had arrived at the hospital and they had wheeled Eddie away. Her reaction had been to let out a long series of imaginative curse words at the 'motherfuckin', low-life dick wads' who had done this to their friend. It was impressive stuff from an eighty-year-old lady, who always dressed like she was on her way to church on Sunday. She had agreed to take Yomi in an instant as she always enjoyed his company. Yomi never displayed any attitude when he was round her place, probably because he didn't want to imagine the tongue-lashing he would get from the old girl if he did.

To his credit, Yomi had been shocked to hear about Eddie, when his father had called them both later to report on the old man's condition. Joseph still had no way of knowing if the incident would put him off the idea of carrying a knife, or merely reinforce his view that they all lived in a horrible place and he would need all the protection he could get. Joseph made himself a sandwich and poured a larger than average glass of whisky. He ate less than half the sandwich then pushed it to one side, too weary to eat it all. Instead, he topped up his glass with a little more Bushmills then stared out of the window wondering how his life in America had ever become so complicated.

The next morning, Joseph got a call on his cell phone from a lady at the hospital who gave him the good news. Eddie was awake and showing no sign of brain damage. 'Unless you include a foul mouth and a sassy attitude with some of my staff,' she told him pointedly. The patient was apparently strong enough to receive visitors, so Joseph went right over there.

When he arrived on the ward, Eddie was sitting up in bed, propped up by two enormous pillows, with his head lolling back like it would involve way too much effort to raise it. He looked all in, too exhausted even to give Joseph some of that famous attitude.

'How you feeling?' Joseph asked his friend.

'How am I feeling?' he repeated it weakly.

'How do you think? Stupid, that's how I'm feeling. Should never have let them creep up behind me like that. They got the drop on me, didn't they? Got a bang to the head and that's all I can remember. Everything else must have happened when I hit the ground.'

'So you didn't get a look at any of them?'

'What did I just say?' snapped Eddie hoarsely. 'They wuz behind me.'

'Okay, take it easy,' said Joseph. 'You want some water?'

Eddie nodded weakly, so Joseph poured him a glass from a large, plastic jug by the side of the bed. He brought the glass up to Eddie's mouth but the old man was forced to raise his head slightly to drink and the effort caused him to wince in pain

'So,' said Eddie, 'you drop by here to say I told you so? That why you came?'

'No, I came here because I was worried about you and I wanted to apologise.'

'Huh?'

'For being late. I'd have been with you if I wasn't running late so, for that, I apologise.'

Eddie didn't seem to know how to respond. Instead he just muttered something unintelligible before adding in a clearer voice, 'Bring any grapes?'

'No.'

'Good, I hate grapes,' was the old man forgiving him in his own way. 'Bring any Bushmills?'

'Eddie, you have a fractured skull and severe concussion.'

'So? What's your point? All the more reason for a drink ain't it?' His testiness was now more in jest. 'So if you ain't brung the whisky, what did you bring?'

Joseph reached into the brown paper grocery bag he was carrying, 'The *New Jersey Observer.*' He knew Eddie liked to keep up with the news from his old neighbourhood. 'Some donuts from Dunkin Doughnuts, and don't worry I didn't get you the Boston Kreme ones, 'cos I know you won't eat them on principle. These are the chocolate-glazed variety.' Didn't all cops in America like doughnuts, reasoned Joseph? Eddie didn't seem too thrilled though. 'And a copy of *I the Jury.*' He handed Eddie a battered old paperback he had found in a second hand store weeks ago and kept forgetting to give to the old guy.

Joseph had expected Eddie's eyes to light up at the sight of his discovery in the local thrift store. Instead he said quietly, 'Mickey Spillane, thanks. I'll be sure and read that one, once my head stops pounding.' Even the thought of the classic tome from his favourite pulp-fiction crime writer, a man who was raised in New Jersey, couldn't snap Eddie out of his low mood.

They talked for a while, but Joseph could see the old man was getting tired and he decided to leave him to get some rest. Eddie was clearly not himself and something made Joseph feel that it wasn't just the physical injuries that had taken their toll on him. Eddie's pride was hurting. He was down, depressed even, though a man of his age and background would never use that word. Something was preying heavily on his mind though. Joseph wasn't sure what it was. Maybe, as he had come round in the hospital bed after his beating, Eddie had been forced to finally face the unpalatable truth that he was getting old.

Joseph had managed to keep his anger in check since the moment he discovered Eddie lying there unconscious by the lockups. Instead, he had been filled with worry for his friend. Now that there seemed every prospect of the old man making a full recovery, that worry had eased a little and was replaced by a deep, brooding anger, directed at whoever it was that had attacked an elderly victim in such a cowardly fashion. It was time to pay someone a visit.

'I need to speak to your son,' he said.

'And who in the hell are you?' asked Mrs Letts folding her thin arms across her bosom defensively.

'Joseph Soyinka. My son Yomi is in the same junior high as Jermaine.'

'Well, I don't see your son here with you, so I guess this ain't no play date.'

Joseph realised that Jermaine Letts mother can't have had things easy. With a no-account, drug-dealing husband and a bunch of children associated with a variety of gangs, petty crimes and now even a murder case, she had clearly not had a stress-free life. The strain of a low-income existence on the periphery of society had prematurely aged her and she seemed to have just one default expression a hard, defiant look, which she directed out against a world she was in seemingly permanent conflict with. Joseph understood all of this, but right now he had no time for her attitude.

'Mrs Letts, I realise you have your problems, but so have I. I just left an old man who's in hospital with a whole bunch of broken bones and a fractured skull,'

'That ain't got nothing to do with my

Jermaine.' She said it without hesitation, too quickly to have even considered whether her son could have been involved. It was the default position of a woman who has been quizzed a thousand times by police officers. It wasn't my child, no, sir.'

'Well, I'm glad you're so sure about that but my friend was attacked outside those lockups at the far end of the project, just a few days after he spoke to your son there and moved him along.'

'Don't prove a thing and you ain't the cops anyhow, elsewise where's your badge?'

'No, you're right, that doesn't mean anything on its own and you're correct that I'm not the cops.'

She seemed inordinately pleased by the admission she had coaxed from him.

'I can see you'd prefer not to deal with me on this matter so I'm going to leave here right now. Then I'm going to drive straight down to the precinct. I will then tell the cops what I just told you and we'll see what they want to do about it, shall we? I understand the guys down there know all about your son already. I hear they only let him out a day or so ago. Guess they'll be real pleased to see him back again. I forgot to add that my friend in the hospital used to be a cop and you know what they're like for looking out for their own. Who knows how they will take the news that Jermaine has been dishing out beatings to retired police-men. I guess they'll make him real welcome when they hear that. Jermaine just better hope the old man doesn't die of his injuries.'

Mrs Letts' face dropped, and when she spoke all the fight had gone out of her voice. 'Well, thing is, he ain't in right now.'

'Really,' said Joseph dryly. 'Then he must have a twin,' and he glanced over her shoulder towards the worried-looking teen-ager standing right behind her.

Mrs Letts turned round and saw her son who said quietly, 'S'okay, Ma, I ain't done nothing.' Jermaine's shoulders were drooped and his eyes were red circles. Whatever the police had put him through, it had left him too exhausted to argue with the stranger at his door.

'Wipe your feet before you come in here,' Mrs Letts told Joseph by way of welcome, leaving the door open as she turned her back on him and padded off into the kitchen.

Jermaine's mother must have been more rattled than he expected by Joseph's threat to involve the police for she even made them a pot of coffee. They all sat round the kitchen table to drink it and Mrs Letts said, 'So, you wanted to speak to my boy. Well, say what you got to say, then think about leaving. You can see how tired he is.'

Joseph leaned forward so he was looking Jermaine right in the eye. 'I just want Jermaine here to explain to me how and why Eddie Filan got such a beating down at the lockups.'

'Wasn't nothing to do with me,' said the boy firmly. 'I know Eddie, known him for ever, I didn't give that old guy no beatin'.'

'You hear that?' Either Mrs Letts assumed Joseph was deaf or she thought her son's word was all that was needed.

'But you were standing guard on those same lockups the other day when he moved you along,' continued Joseph.

Jermaine glanced at his mother and Joseph said, 'She isn't going to answer for you, Jermaine. I know you were there, Eddie told me, said he'd cut you some slack.'

'I guess,' conceded the boy and he looked down at his training shoes.

Immediately, Mrs Letts attitude changed. 'Hell you doin' that for, Jermaine. You promised me you'd have nothing to do with no gangs. You promised your momma!'

Jermaine continued to stare down at the ground, a tough young boy cowed into submission by this tiny woman.

'So Eddie let you off the hook and this is how you repay him?' continued Joseph. 'The next time he appears at the lockups, you and your gang jump him and smash his skull in.'

'No!' said Jermaine vehemently.

'Tell me you didn't do it! Swear to your momma!' Mrs Letts was getting riled up now. It was a distraction Joseph could do without, but her disapproval might just help him to break down the boy's resistance.

'What you hit him with, Jermaine, a baseball bat?' asked Joseph, matter of factly.

'No, I never...' He was shaking his head from side to side.

'Did it make you feel like a big man? Smashing an old guy's skull in and leaving him to bleed all over the ground like that?'

'Oh, sweet Jesus!' called his mother, clasping her hands to her face then turning her eyes to heaven. 'After all I told you about your good for nothing father, you go and start a gang.' Jermaine was still shaking his head vehemently, but his mother had taken his admission that he was a lookout as proof positive he was mixed up in the whole affair.

'How could you do this to your momma?'

Suddenly, and to Joseph's astonishment, tears began to flow from Jermaine's eyes and his voice became distorted by sobs that made his whole body convulse. 'I didn't, I didn't. Stop it, please. Leave me alone. I didn't hit Eddie and I didn't stab that teacher, neither.' The tears rolled down his face. 'Why won't anybody believe me? Stop saying it. Just leave me alone!'

The strain of the relentless interrogations into the Lopez murder, followed by the probing from Joseph and his mother, must have brought Jermaine to breaking point. The boy seemed to regress into a small child right there in front of them and it took a full minute before his sobbing finally subsided, eventually turning into a pitiful whimper. One thing Joseph was now certain of. This was no gang leader.

Jermaine's mother seemed shocked at the sight, then her face took on a new emotion, guilt at having doubted her son. To hide her shame and confusion she rounded on Joseph. 'You happy now?' she demanded.

'Just a moment,' he told her, then turned his attention back to the boy's tear-streaked face. 'Okay, Jermaine, I believe you, I really do. So who did it then? Who could do such a cowardly thing to a frail, old man?'

Jermaine just shook his head.

'Come on, this is Eddie we're talking about here,' and the boy seemed to get even more upset. He clammed up and was silent for a while, head down, face screwed up as he tried to stifle the tears. Joseph was just about to give up when Jermaine finally spoke, and when he did the words came out in a rush.

'It's not my fault, I didn't want to go. It was Macy Williams' fault. If it weren't for her...'

'Macy Williams?' asked Joseph incredulously. 'What's she got to do with this?'

'Rihanna...' he whispered

'Who's Rihanna?' and when he received no reply he looked at Mrs Letts.

'My daughter...' she admitted, though she was guarded again now that another family member could be implicated. Joseph recalled the girl at her side during the parents' meeting.

'She cut Macy out of the gang,' said Jermaine, 'so they was one short. She made me watch out instead.'

Joseph nodded, for he understood it all now. Jermaine Letts wasn't the leader of the gang that had beaten up Eddie. It was Rihanna Letts. The gang leader was a girl.

12

They brought Eddie back late morning but he was a different man. Gone was the wise-ass humour and bantering comebacks of Eddie in a good mood. Gone too was the cantankerous foul mouth of Eddie in a bad mood. Joseph missed that almost as much. In its place was a listless, old man who wasn't interested in anything. He was helped into bed, still wearing the pyjamas Marjorie had found somewhere amid the disordered chaos of his bedroom. She had laundered them and Joseph had brought them down to the hospital for Eddie, so he would have something clean to wear on his journey home.

They propped him up with pillows stuffed behind his back then surrounded him with items at arm's reach, which he studiously ignored. Books, magazines, candy and messages from a handful of well-wishers were barely glanced at, even the card from Yomi. He quietly turned down all offers of food and non-alcoholic drink. Instead, he stared off into the middle distance of his apartment window, contemplating the sky intently, as if he was sure something interesting might fall from it at any moment.

When he communicated with Joseph and Marjorie at all it was only to answer their most direct of questions with a single word.

'You okay, honey?' asked the concerned old lady.

'Yeah.'

'Can we get you anything?'

'No,' pronounced nyaah with strangled Jersey vowels.

'You want the radio on?' Joseph asked but the question didn't seem to even warrant a reply.

Eventually, Marjorie asked, 'You sure you don't want me to fetch some of my soup?' and she finally received a sentence from him.

'Quit fussing over me, woman, goddamit,' he growled.

'Normally I'd have torn you a new asshole for that,' she told him calmly, 'but you been beat up bad enough already. I'll come by again later, see if you in a better mood. Come on, Joseph.' And they left Eddie alone with his thoughts.

'He didn't badger us once for a sip of Irish whisky,' said the old woman confidentially in the corridor. 'Things must be bad.'

167

She was right, thought Joseph. He hadn't and they were.

His old Lago friend Cyrus was waiting for him down at the Impala with a huge, toothy grin and a bottle of cold beer. It was an appointment he could do without right now, but Cyrus had said he had a proposition to put to his friend. Joseph thought he'd better turn up to make sure it wasn't some damn fool idea that would get them both in trouble. Cyrus attracted trouble, like horse-shit attracts flies.

'Joseph, my brother!' he called and waved the bottle of beer at his friend. Joseph waved back and crossed the floor. As always, the Impala was full of off-duty taxi drivers, minimum-wage hotel workers and barmen on a break, all spending their tips on a little bit of West African food to remind them of the home they had left behind. Joseph hadn't thought he was hungry when he walked in but that soon changed when he passed a table filled with plates of Ikokore, boiled yams cooked with dried fish in tomatoes and palm oil, and Ewa, the soft beans made with onions and peppers. Oh how the Impala reminded him of home with its bittersweet memories of the meals Apara had prepared for him. That was another life and it seemed so long ago.

When he reached Cyrus, his friend got to his feet and embraced him. 'It's good to see you, my brother. Tonight we eat together and this time it is all on me, Joseph. I knew you would protest, which is why I have ordered already, so I am very glad you are on time. They are bringing us pancakes and beef Suya with Jollof rice.'

'That's generous of you, Cyrus,' answered Joseph doubtfully, 'but I don't think I can let you buy me dinner, unless you finally went on Jeopardy and won.'

Cyrus laughed. He was always telling everybody that would listen how easy it would be to get rich on American game shows.

'There's no need for that, my friend. I'm doing pretty good now and it's all thanks to my new job, which is why I wanted to speak to you.' Cyrus Agyeman had gone up in the world. No longer a cab driver, these days he liked to refer to himself as the concierge of a small hotel in Mott Haven, though in reality he actually worked for the real concierge. These days, he wore a dark suit and tie, even here in the Impala. He had already explained to Joseph how he was the linkman to out-oftowners and the things they desired from a business trip. 'If they want it, I can get it for them,' he would say confidentially. 'Except drugs,' he then added quickly for Joseph's benefit. 'Drugs I don't get for anybody, not ever, but tickets for a show, perhaps even a girl... maybe...' He shrugged and smiled self-consciously. A little over a year ago, Cyrus had almost been sent away for life when the local drug lord tried to frame him for murder. Joseph had managed to get him off the hook and Cyrus had never stopped thanking him for it. He thought he owed his friend, big style. For Joseph it was different. Cyrus had been the only friend he had when he arrived in America with a young son and precious little else. It was Cyrus who had found him a job, got him in front of the right people for the apartment. Joseph reckoned they were about even.

'The man I told you about, my manager at the hotel, he's a good guy, not a crook. I mean, maybe he doesn't pay all of his taxes but he isn't a gangster, you know what I mean,' confided Cyrus. 'Anyhow, he likes me. Why? Because I work hard and we make money together. The hotel pay us to take care of the guests, then we put them into things, hire cars, cabs sometimes.' He gave Joseph a significant look. 'Then there's restaurants, Broadway shows, gambling and if they want a little company ... we provide all the things men want when they are in town on business. What their wives don't see...' He grinned at the sheer nerve of some of the hotel's guests. 'Anyway, all this action don't come cheap. The guests pay good money for these entertainments and since we are the ones who get to send them places, those places pay us for recommending them. This guy I work for, he's in with all the top managers at the hotels. They trust him. So he gets to put a new concierge in a hotel from our group when one of them leaves and a job becomes vacant and do you know what?'

'What?'

'One just left.' Cyrus was smiling again. 'Which means he's looking for a good man. Since there is a shortage of good men in New York City, this isn't as easy as you might think. My manager wants someone discreet, who will work hard and isn't too greedy. He needs someone who'll kick a fair share of the money back to him, not try and keep it all for himself like some guys do. He asked me if I knew anyone and I told him all about my friend Joseph. He is honest I say, you can trust Joseph. Well, he was very happy to hear that and now he wants to meet you.'

'I don't know, Cyrus.' His friend meant well but Cyrus was really asking him to become a kind of pimp, receiving kickbacks from hookers and gambling dens in exchange for a steady stream of customers from his hotel. It wasn't the job Joseph had exactly dreamed off when he first came to America but then neither was taxi driver.

'Why not?' Cyrus was frowning at him like he was a fool. 'You know how many hours you got to do in the cab to make the kind of money I'm on? And it's not illegal, not really. I told this guy I wouldn't get blow for anyone and he's cool with it. Anyone wants blow he says get them to call him direct and he'll send someone down but I don't get involved in any of that. So who are we hurting, really? Huh?'

'I'm still working on this NYPD application and...'

'Aw, come on, Joseph, forget all that,' said his friend wearily. 'You know they never gonna let you join their police force. Americans think every Nigerian is involved in a 419 scam.' Cyrus was probably right about that. Their country had become infamous worldwide for all of the wrong reasons, chief among them the 419 advance fee fraud, so called because of the number of its listing as an offence in the Nigerian Criminal Code. The 419 scam had been a form of local irritation to the police and the unwitting victims of the confidence tricksters for years, but the idea really only took off with the advent of e-mail and the Internet. Now confidence tricksters were free to spam the globe looking for the gullible, who were tricked into advancing money, as a tax on a non-existent lottery win or to assist in the laundering of a fictitious dictator's money or the transportation of a US soldier's booty of foreign gold bullion, from which a huge share was always promised in exchange for just a little assistance. The victims would then either lose the money they'd sent or foolishly open up the details of their bank accounts, which would then be ruthlessly plundered. It was amazing how many idiots there were who would believe these outlandish tales they were sent. How quickly greed turned men into fools. Fortunes were made on the backs of those unthinking idiots and Nigeria had become known as the spiritual capital of the e-mail confidence trick, to Joseph's eternal shame.

'In any case,' concluded Cyrus. 'You told

me you can't get a reference.'

Joseph couldn't deny he was right on that score. It seemed the New York Police Department were unlikely to be contacting him any time soon and he was becoming mightily sick of driving a cab round the poorer parts of the city, trying to eke out a living. Maybe Cyrus was right. Perhaps it was time to earn some easy money, carrying bags for businessmen and having hookers on speed dial. Cyrus continued to extol the virtues of his job, his new-found comparative wealth and the level of cool his boss exhibited at all times, just so long as the money came in and was kicked back. It seemed there was more than enough for everyone.

'I'll have to think about it, Cyrus,' concluded Joseph when their food arrived. 'But I will do that, I promise,'

'Okay, but don't leave it too long. He'll find someone else if you do.'

Cyrus was in a good mood and while they ate, all of the stories of their time in the old country came back to him, to be dusted off and repeated with enthusiasm, complete with wild embellishments. Most of them involved the scrapes Cyrus had got himself mixed up in, many of which he admitted he would have had difficulty extricating himself from, if it had not been for his oldest, finest friend, Joseph Soyinka.

Eventually the talk came round to Yomi, and Joseph admitted the boy was giving him a hard time these days. Cyrus listened carefully while Joseph explained the difficulties he was having with his son, concluding with his surly manner and belligerent attitude of late. To Joseph's surprise, his friend started to smile and by the end of Joseph's story the smile had turned into a chuckle.

'You mind telling me what's so damn funny?' asked Joseph, a little annoyed at not being taken seriously.

'You are,' said Cyrus. 'The great detective and you cannot see what's right at the end of your nose.'

'What do you mean?'

'You don't know why Yomi is acting the way he is right now? Seriously?'

'I suppose you think you do?'

Cyrus nodded. 'Girls,' he said simply.

'Girls?'

Was his friend serious? Did Cyrus really think his son was carrying a knife around because of girls?

'Sure. Have you forgotten what it's like to be that age? Can't you remember what we talked about back then?' Joseph had to admit that he could not. 'Believe me,' continued Cyrus, 'that was pretty much the only thing we talked about as I remember. That and football, maybe, but girls mostly. Who was the best girl in the class, the prettiest girl in the street, the cutest girl in the whole school, our part of Lagos, the whole damn world. Don't you remember?'

'No, not really,' Joseph conceded.

'It was our whole life, man. How do we get to meet them, be alone with them, ask them out, ever get to kiss them. It was everything.' He was laughing at the memory. 'Man, we'd have murdered each other to see a bare breast, just one, one would have done. Not even a pair!' Joseph was baffled. Was he really that concerned by the opposite sex at that age? He had vague recollections of wanting to play football or become a racing driver, but he seemed to have airbrushed those early yearnings for the fairer sex out of his memories. Cyrus though seemed to remember everything. 'We even talked about drilling a hole in the wall of the girls' locker rooms so we could watch them change for swimming. We'd have done it, too, if we hadn't been too damned scared of getting caught. Oh my, I can't believe you've forgotten all that.'

'Well, I'm afraid I have, Cyrus. But what's

all that got to do with Yomi's behaviour?'

'Because women do that to you, man. They get you all riled up, so you don't know what you doing. They get you so you can't think straight. You do stupid things to impress them, even though they usually ain't impressed at all. You said Yomi showed his knife to some girls, yes?'

'Yes.'

'There you go. He was trying to impress them.'

'But he's never said a word.'

'Did you tell your old man when you started liking girls?'

'I guess not. So you think Yomi's a little crazy right now because of females?'

'Yeah, that's all, but you don't have to worry so much because he'll grow out of it. Everyone does.'

This was some consolation. 'You think so?'

'Sure, I did,' said Cyrus dismissively. 'I used to get into all kinds of scrapes when I was his age but look at me now. I turned out all right in the end.'

This wasn't the kind of assurance Joseph was looking for. Cyrus had turned out all right in the end by his standards of maturity. Along the way he'd been caught up in troubles that would have given a less-optimistic man grey hair and stomach ulcers. Joseph drained the last mouthful of his drink and glanced at his watch. 'I've got to be going.'

'Poor old Joseph,' said Cyrus, leaning back in his chair like he had all the time in the world. 'Always rushing round and running off somewhere.'

'Yeah, and this time I'm gonna be late.'

'Why, you got a hot date or something?'

'Not exactly.' But he did have an appointment with a woman.

Joseph put the last tin can up on the middle shelf and stepped back so she could survey his work. He knew she liked everything to be 'just-so', as she called it.

'You're an angel sent from god,' said Marjorie. 'Everything's in its place and there is a place for everything.' She smiled at Joseph. The old lady made them some coffee and motioned for Joseph to sit down. 'Thank you for getting my groceries, Joseph,' she said. 'I don't know how things'd be without you fetching and carrying for me all the time.'

'And I don't know how I'd get along if you didn't watch over Yomi for me like you do when I need it.'

'It ain't like I got anywhere else to be.' The

178

old lady took a moment to lower herself into her chair. 'Now when Yomi drops by next time I can make him some of my pancakes. He likes my pancakes.'

'You spoil my boy, Marjorie,' he told the old lady. 'And don't go thinking he's hungry when you go feeding him. More than likely he'll have had his dinner with me just an hour before. Don't know where he puts all the food he gets.'

'He's a growing boy, got to feed him up. He's growing up fast, too. Won't be too long before he gets his'self a girlfriend, I shouldn't wonder.'

'That's exactly what my friend Cyrus has just been saying but I don't think so, not Yomi. He's not shown any interest in girls just yet.'

'Huh, like he'd tell his daddy if he had. He won't want you to know in case you make fun of him. And don't think I don't hear you and that no-account Eddie Filan teasing that poor boy 'bout all manner of things. I tell you something, if I was a boy and I liked a girl I wouldn't tell you all till I was growed up and we was engaged!' and she laughed.

'I hadn't thought of it like that,' he admitted, 'but I don't think he's too interested, really I don't.'

'How has he been since this teacher of his got stabbed, god rest the poor mother-fucker.' Try as he might, Joseph could never get used to the old girl's foul language, the words coming as they did from the mouth of a lady who looked like she could be a great grandmother.

'He seems okay I guess,' said Joseph, 'and that's what worries me. He and his friends seem to have just accepted it and moved on. I mean, they're sorry and all but they're acting like it's just one of those things.'

'Maybe it is round these parts,' she said. 'I guess you become hardened to that sort of thing when you live in Highbridge long enough.' Which was exactly what was bothering Joseph. If Yomi could shrug off a brutal murder at the age of twelve then what would he be like by the time he was in his late teens. And, if Highbridge was that bad, how in the hell was he going to get them both out of there before it got any worse?

'I dropped by on Eddie while you were out, to see how he was managing.' she said. 'He told me you'd been thinking a lot about what happened at the school, trying to figure out who'd want to murder that teacher. You know what I think?'

'No, but I'd be glad to hear it.'

'Well, now I ain't no detective,' proclaimed Marjorie, 'but I watch a lot of that stuff on the TV.'

'You do, huh?'

'Oh yeah, always have done. There's reruns *of Kojak* and *Columbo* during the day time and the *Rockford Files* with James Garner. I like him, he's tall.' She smiled knowingly. 'Then in the night there's *CSI* and all those cold-case documentaries about serial killers and shit. A lot of them is fucked in the head, they can't help it 'cos they born that way. We should pity 'em before we locks 'em away for ever and throws away the key.' Marjorie then embarked on a massive coughing fit that went on for so long, Joseph began to feel genuinely concerned for her wellbeing, until she finally cleared her throat and said, 'Then there's the other kind of killer.'

'What kind is that?'

'Someone with a reason to kill. That makes it easier for the cops.'

'How so?' he asked her.

'You find the reason,' she said confidently, 'and you found your killer.'

He couldn't deny there was a lot of truth in that. 'And what reason do you suppose anyone would have for getting into a school at night and stabbing some poor teacher to death?'

'Well, I can't say I know anything about that,' she said, 'but there's usually pretty much only two motives for killing someone, according to what I seen on the TV.'

'And what are they?'

'Money and fucking.'

Joseph laughed. 'Is that what it all boils down to do you think, Marjorie? Simple as that, huh?'

'Yep, 'bout as simple as that. Nearly every killing you can name basically been caused because of money and fucking.' She thought for a time. 'Oh and religion, but that there is a whole different thing all together. Someone loves his god so much he just has to go and kill you for loving a different one, well that is almost as fucked up as them serial killers. It ain't a real reason.' She hauled herself to her feet and went off to fetch a plate of Oreos she had left on the counter top. 'Normal people, though, when they kill, well, like I say, you don't usually got to look too far beyond money and fucking to find the reason why.'

13

The internet café had opened up just a few doors along from the Impala, with a ready eye on its clientele. There were a number of small businesses in the same street that had all sprung up at roughly the same time primarily to service the growing band of migrant workers who craved a link to their homeland. The same workers who came here for the Impala's authentic food were now tempted by a store that sold traditional ingredients for African meals, a broker who could arrange the transfer of money to foreign bank accounts and a business that sold international time on its phones so you could call home to loved ones, a service Joseph knew he would never need.

The Internet café had brightly lit, orange-painted walls and four rows of computers lined up in front of an Espresso machine, which sat behind a long counter filled with plates of cakes and brownies that had cheap, plastic domes over them to protect their produce. Joseph purchased some credit, politely declined the opportunity to buy some coffee and a muffin, the blueberry was on special, then chose a computer in a quiet corner of the room. The handful of other users ignored him as he passed between them. They all had their heads down over their keyboards, typing out e-mails that were for the most part destined for hotmail accounts in Africa and East Asia. He chose a computer and switched it on, opened up a search-engine page from Google and typed in the words 'McIndoe Campaign'.

Joseph ignored the references to US corporations of the same name and he passed over the amateur blogs from similar-sounding high school girls, who assumed the world was interested in their adolescent musings. Instead he went straight to the home page of the McIndoe campaign's founder and read the blurb that accompanied a photograph, to satisfy himself that this was indeed what he was looking for. It was all as he had remembered it from reports in the media. Joseph took out a pen and jotted the contact phone number onto a piece of scrap paper then carefully folded it and put it in his pocket. He would make the call later, in private, where no one could overhear his plan. This was a move he would not take lightly. In America they would probably call it 'Tough Love'.

'Come in, Yomi,' said Joseph as his son entered their apartment. 'There's someone I'd like you to meet.'

'Hello, Yomi,' said the middle-aged, black lady kindly. 'Why don't you come over here and sit down.' She had dressed smartly for their appointment and was obviously not expecting it to be a long one, for she had kept on her immaculate coat, with its shiny, gold brooch shaped like a Gecko, that was pinned to one of its big lapels. She had on a pair of new gloves, which she finally took off as she spoke, neatly folding them and placing them on top of her handbag.

'What's going on?' asked Yomi, immediately suspicious of this newcomer.

'Your daddy asked me to come here for a little talk with you after school,' she said, in a voice that personified calm.

'Who are you?' demanded Yomi, his anxiety betrayed by the slightly higher than normal pitch of his voice. 'Dad, who is this?'

Joseph stayed silent and the woman said, 'My name is Eloise McIndoe but that won't mean anything to you.'

'You some kind of social worker, come

down here to scare me. Is that what this is?' asked Yomi. Once again he sounded far older than his years. Joseph found himself wondering where his son was getting his ideas from lately.

'I'm not a social worker, no.' She said it so placidly that Joseph couldn't help but marvel at this woman's strength and resolve.

'Psychiatrist then,' taunted Yomi, 'come to see one of the bad kids? I've heard about that, too.' He said it sullenly and his father was close to intervening now but Eloise simply gave Yomi a disarming little smile, as if he had said something quite unimportant in the scheme of things.

'No, I'm just a nobody really. My name was in all the papers once, but only for a short while and not for anything I did.'

That seemed to intrigue Yomi. 'Why was that?' he asked.

'Would you like to see a picture of my son?' She smiled pleasantly, ignoring his question. 'From when he was around your age?'

Yomi shrugged, trying to look as if he really didn't care one way or another, but he was already finding it hard to act coldly towards this lady. Needing no further bidding, she opened up the clip on her handbag and drew out a handful of photographs then placed them face down on her knee. Then she paused and looked up again, giving Yomi a questioning look, as if to say 'you don't really expect a lady to get up and bring them over do you?'

God she was good, thought Joseph. She could convey all that in the merest glance and Yomi was already moving, like he was compelled to go to her. He sat on the threadbare couch next to her.

'That's Francis just after his thirteenth birthday,' and she handed him the first picture. From where Joseph was standing, he could just see the image of the smiling boy in his school photograph, bashful but carefree. It was the same picture Eloise McIndoe used on her website.

Yomi took the photo uncertainly, not knowing what he was supposed to make of it but Eloise was not waiting for a response, she was already on to the next photograph. 'And this is Francis a year or so later with his daddy and his granddaddy. They off to the ball game together.'

Yomi surveyed the picture of three generations of the McIndoe clan and, in the absence of anything else to say, he settled on a softly spoken 'cool' in deference to the other boy's obvious love of baseball.

'He and his daddy were real close.'

Yomi looked a little alarmed there for he couldn't fail to pick-up on her use of the past tense. You could see him praying that it was the father or the granddaddy, who was no longer with them and not the son.

Then, with no obvious change of pace or inflection, Eloise dropped the bombshell. 'And this is a photograph of my little boy's gravestone. He was fifteen years old when he died.'

She didn't hand the picture to Yomi this time, that would have been too much, but she had definitely got his full attention now. His eyes widened and he froze, a picture of discomfort. Joseph could tell he was trying to work out what to say in reply that wouldn't offend this poor lady, but he needn't have worried. Eloise was content to do all of the talking. 'I go down there most days. I guess some of my friends and neighbours must think that's a little strange or morbid and maybe it is but, to tell you the truth Yomi, when you have lost your only child like I did, well there ain't much more to life anymore than tending to his grave and being as close to him as I can. So I go down there and I sit on the bench by his grave and I talk to my boy, tell him how much I miss him.'

'Sorry,' mumbled Yomi, his head down, unable to look her in the eye.

'You don't have to be sorry, son,' she said, still using the same calm and measured tone. 'Weren't your fault he died,' and with that she put her photographs back together and placed them carefully in the handbag and did up the clasp. 'You won't have heard of my boy. He wasn't around long enough to make that much of a mark on the world, but he was a real nice kid with a good heart and he sure loved his momma, I know it and 1 take some comfort from that.' Yomi looked like he hardly dared to breathe. 'His grades were okay and I think he'd have made his way if he'd graduated from high school like we planned. Thing is he never got the chance. Do you know what happened to him?'

'No,' the word was barely a whisper.

'His friend killed him.'

'His friend?' asked Yomi incredulously.

'Uh-huh, you see they had a fight, like young boys do. You've had fights with your friends ain't ya?'

'I guess, sometimes.'

'Trouble was, when they had their fight, Francis' friend, he had a knife. He also had a temper and he stabbed my poor little boy right through the heart before he had time to even think about what he was doing. My Francis died right there in the street. By the time I reached him, he was lying there lifeless on the pavement. I didn't even get to hold him before he passed away.'

Yomi's face told Joseph everything he needed to know. His mouth fell open and his eyes were glued to Eloise. She was still talking in that same cool, calm and measured tone, like she could have been describing her bus journey over to their apartment. 'The judge said it was a heat of the moment thing, like his friend snapped without thinking of the consequences. Just like that.' She snapped her fingers and Yomi visibly jumped. 'He said it was a tragedy for two families and I know he was right because I saw my son's friend's momma weeping in the dock when they sent him to the penitentiary. I never want to see another woman crying like that again as long as I live. Francis' friend is called Edward. He was the same age as my boy and they say, if he is real lucky, he may get out of the state correctional facility, that's a fancy word for prison, when he is just over thirty years old. I try not to think about the unspeakable things they are probably doing to that boy in there. Most of all, I try every day not to wish them on him. Revenge is a very human thing to want, Yomi, but it has a way of eating you up inside, consuming the person you used to be, you understand me? Anyways, I guess there's two young boys whose lives were ended right there and then when that knife came out.'

Yomi was rigid, unblinking. 'Know what I do now?' she asked. ''Part from tending my poor little boy's grave? Well, I'll tell you. I go round the schools in the neighbourhood with my project, which is to tell all the children what happened to my Francis and how easy it was for him to die on account of how his friend was carrying a knife when they had a stupid argument about nothing.' Yomi looked terrified, for he knew what was coming next. It was all the more chilling for the way in which Eloise voice never faltered, never left the slight sing-song, reasonable-as-hell tone of a mother, who sounded as if she was asking her son if he had been a naughty boy and eaten an extra cookie from the jar without asking. 'Your daddy called me up this morning and he asked if I'd come over and speak to you, Yomi. He says you been carrying a knife lately. Is that true?' Tears welled up in Yomi's eyes then, and he nodded miserably. 'Well I hope after our little talk you'll do me a very great personal favour. Would you do that for me, sugar?'

He looked up and asked, 'What?'

'Promise me you won't do that again, will you? It would mean a lot to me to know it 'cos I'd hate to hear one day about your daddy getting a call like the one I got, telling him you'd been killed like my little boy. It'd be no consolation to him if he got to spend the next fifteen years counting the days till they release you from a growed-up man's prison for killing some other boy, neither. I don't want to imagine what that poor boy's momma is going through. After all she didn't do nothing to me or my poor boy, yet she suffers, every day, too, just the same as me. Will you look me in the eye and promise me you won't pick-up a knife again, honey?'

And Yomi did look her in the eye and he did promise and this time Joseph was sure that he meant it.

'Thank you, sugar,' she said simply and she rose to her feet. 'I'll see myself out, Joseph,' and she waved her hand at him when he tried to thank her. 'Oh, shush now. I'm here for my own benefit too. Only thing gets me to the end of each day is the thought that someone might listen to what I got to say from time to time and maybe even do something about it afterwards. Goodbye, Yomi, it was nice meeting you. You be a good boy for your daddy, you hear.' And with that she was gone.

Yomi was very quiet that night and he went to bed early. Only a few words had passed between them by the time Joseph drove his son back to Antoinette Irving the next morning. Before they reached the old school building, his son finally spoke.

'Could we pull over here?'

'You got something you want to say to me?' asked Joseph.

When Yomi nodded, his father drew up the car by the side of the road a few hundred metres from the school gates.

'I never said I was ashamed of you,' Yomi said.

'What?'

'For being a cab driver. I never said I was ashamed of you. I'm not ashamed of you.' He was looking straight ahead.

'Okay, then I'm sorry,' said his father. 'I guess I was having a bad day when I said that.'

Yomi nodded slowly, like he understood and accepted the explanation. It didn't look as if he needed to discuss it further.

'Shall we get going then?' asked Joseph.

'Would you mind if I get out here and walk the rest of the way?'

'Why do you want to do that?' Joseph would have been tempted to ask if Yomi was ashamed of his old man, had it not been for the fact he had just told him the opposite. Yomi just shrugged like it was no big deal either way, so his father acquiesced. 'Okay.'

Without another word, Yomi eased himself out of the cab and went quietly off towards the school. Joseph stayed behind the wheel of his car and watched his son go. It had been a relief to hear his son say it, but the words that passed between them that morning had not entirely put his mind at rest. Joseph was sure Yomi meant it when he had promised never to carry a knife again, but this getting out of the cab a few blocks from school for no apparent reason was strange behaviour and it made Joseph feel uneasy. He watched as Yomi selected a side street and turned down it and, before he could rationalise the act, Joseph found that he was climbing out of the cab and had begun to follow his son.

Joseph wasn't too worried about being spotted, after all he had tailed professional criminals all over Lagos without being compromised, but he did feel a smattering of guilt distrusting his son like this. Still, he needed to get to the bottom of Yomi's odd behaviour. On the surface it looked like a simple case of truancy, albeit a blatant one.

Yomi wasn't hard to follow for he never looked back, even once. Instead he ambled along the side road near the school until he reached a concrete walkway, which dissected the two playing fields. It was there that he stopped and waited, watched by his father who had taken up a position that afforded him a perfect view of his son's movements. Thanks to the fortuitous positioning of a large advertising hoarding, which towered above him and overlooked the major road nearby, he remained unseen. Joseph stood behind a large metal stanchion and watched as his son suddenly turned and gave a shy wave to an unseen friend. His father waited to see who was going to join Yomi and, more importantly, whether they would be going in to school together or heading off in the opposite direction.

Joseph expected to see FJ come round the corner, so he was completely taken aback when the blurred figure in the middle distance turned out to have long brown hair and was wearing a skirt, for Yomi was meeting a girl. Joseph peered intently at the two of them and was pretty sure that it was Merve Williams' youngest girl who was walking towards Yomi. Yep, it was Laura all right and if his eyes hadn't deceived him, his son had just greeted the girl with a kiss. Now she was kissing his boy back. Joseph immediately felt like he shouldn't be watching this display of private, tender affection and he took a step back, intending to walk away. The last he saw of Laura and Yomi, the two of them were happily holding hands and walking off to school together.

So that's why Yomi had been so keen to get out of the car early. He had a girlfriend and he didn't want his father to know about it. Joseph shook his head. Cyrus had tried to tell him, Marjorie knew it would happen, but Joseph couldn't see it coming at all, and he was supposed to be the detective. As he returned to the cab, he decided to give Yomi a break. There would be no teasing, no questions and no pressure from his father. As far as he was concerned, Yomi could get out of the car early every morning, if all he was doing was meeting a nice girl like Laura. In his view, girls were usually a damn sight less dangerous than knives.

Joseph stared intently at the figure lying beneath him on the cold, hard floor. The dirty, scuffed boots were all that could be seen of the man and they had not moved for some time. Joseph was worried. Suddenly there was a clang and a sharp metallic ring from beneath the vehicle, as a spanner slipped and hit something hard, immediately followed by a muffled curse. Selwyn Wray slid out from under the jacked-up taxi with a frown across his face and a small stripe of fresh blood on his finger.

'Cocksuckin', motherfuckin' whore,' he said with some conviction, staring at the car accusingly as he wedged his hand under an armpit and winced in pain. Selwyn examined his finger and, satisfied that the damage was minor, wiped the blood onto his filthy overalls before turning his attention back to the yellow cab. Selwyn then fell into the kind of silent contemplation that would have impressed a Buddhist monk, continuing to stare at the offending vehicle, as if the answer to his conundrum was written across its bonnet.

'Well?' asked Joseph when he could take the silence no more.

'If she was a horse, I'd shoot her,' said Selwyn in disgust.

'Please don't say that.'

'Okay,' conceded the mechanic reasonably. 'If she was my wife I'd kick her scrawny ass out the door,' and he wiped the grease from his hands with a cloth. 'Sound any better to ya?'

Joseph sighed. 'Well I cannot leave her or shoot her. She's my meal ticket.' He liked to use the American expressions he picked up from his passengers. It made him feel less like an outsider.

'You sure you can't just replace her? Save money in the long run.' Joseph gave Selwyn a look. 'Okay, okay, I'm just asking here.' He pronounced the word 'axeing', betraying his Brooklyn routes.

'I'm still trying to raise the money but a new Crown Victoria is not cheap. Ford don't give them away. I'm leasing the medallion as it is.' Joseph didn't want to admit he had been quietly hoping there would be no need for a new cab. He had planned to sell the old one once his application for the NYPD had gone through, but now he realised the cab was likely to be a worthless pile of scrap metal long before that day came. Then there was the offer from Cyrus' boss who wanted to turn Joseph into his new concierge. Though he still had his reservations, the prospect of a little easier money was beginning to sound more appealing by the day. He was still mulling it over but he knew he would have to call Cyrus with a decision one way or another before too long.

Selwyn exhaled, perused the cab once more and asked, 'What are you gonna do?'

Joseph knew this was a rhetorical question but he had to know the truth. 'I don't know, my friend, what *am* I going to do?'

'I can get you back on the road,' said Selwyn eventually. Relief flooded through Joseph. 'For now,' added the mechanic, bringing Joseph right back down to earth. 'But I gotta tell you, I'm putting a band aid on a heart-attack victim here, you know what I'm saying?'

There was no need to elaborate further. The taxi was on its very last legs. It was now just a question of whether Joseph could scrape enough money together in time to get a new cab before this 'second-hand, second-rate, heap of shit', as Selwyn cheerfully referred to it, finally went off to 'the great big old junk yard in the sky'.

Thank god Selwyn was the one mechanic in the South Bronx he could trust not to rip him off. The two men agreed a fair price for that morning's work, though it was still a stretch for Joseph.

'Get a cup of coffee,' said Selwyn. 'Come back in an hour.' He thought for a moment. 'Better make it two.'

'Okay,' Joseph had anticipated some down time while the cab was being repaired, which was why he had paid another visit to Ardo that morning. He had borrowed the janitor's keys once more, promising faithfully that this would be the very last time, leaving Ardo with an assurance that what he was trying to prove would benefit the little Armenian, eventually removing him from any suspicion from the eyes of a baffled police force. 'Say,' he asked Selwyn, 'do you know any place round here where I could get some keys cut?'

'Sure.'

'Within walking distance?'

'That narrows it down. Is it just your apartment key?'

'Well, that's just it,' answered Joseph guardedly, for he knew Selwyn to be the kind of man who, if not exactly a criminal himself was at least someone who had to be tolerant of criminal goings on in his neighbourhood. Many of his regular clientele could be described as being far from law abiding and, in his own words, Selwyn 'knew how to keep his mouth shut'. He had to when most of his customers were from Highbridge and the surrounding area.

'I need to get a new set of these cut,' and he showed Selwyn Ardo's bunch of keys. 'It's for a friend, only he's lost his card.'

'Sure,' said Selwyn, his face betraying no emotion as he took in the heavy clump of official-looking keys that Joseph held up in front of him. 'I'd say you could try Tony De Luca's parts yard but ... er ... a job like that ain't cheap, Joseph, you know what I mean.'

'That's okay, my friend will pay.'

'Sure,' mumbled Selwyn once again, in a tone that said it's none of my business and he gave his customer directions to Tony De Luca's parts yard. 'It's on the corner where Washington meets E167th.' And about half a mile from Antoinette Irving Junior High School, thought Joseph.

He was about to leave when Pete Hunio, Selwyn's young apprentice, pulled up sharply in an old Ford Mustang, tyres screeching on the oil-coated floor.

'How many times I got to tell you 'bout driving in here like that? You think you're Steve McfuckingQueen?' said Selwyn. 'You want to flatten some poor prick, so his widow sues me and puts us out of business? What you gonna do then, huh?'

'Sorry, boss,' said Pete, grinning like a simpleton.

'And what's this?'

'Owner had an argument with a Lexus on the Cross Bronx, wants the dent knocked out the driver's door,' explained Pete. 'Said he ain't in no hurry but can it be today.' He raised his eyebrows at the contradiction.

Selwyn bent down to examine the dent. 'What do you know about that, Joseph?'

Joseph peered at the damage, 'Paint's been scraped off above the dent right below the window.' He pointed to the fresh abrasions on the bodywork. 'Looks like it was forced.' He walked round to the front of the car. 'Plus the car's old and dirty but theses plates are new and clean. I'd say they were added this morning and this Mustang is stolen.'

Selwyn regarded his friend sharply and Joseph realised too late that all he really wanted was an opinion on the damage. 'Well ain't you a regular Clarice Starling?' There was suspicion behind the words. 'What are you? A cop in your spare time?'

Joseph shrugged and gave the broad smile he always used when he wanted to disarm people. He'd been stupid to let his guard down and immediately regretted it. Only his friend Cyrus, Brigitte and Eddie really knew about his previous life. He preferred it that way but now he'd been sloppy. Sometimes he just couldn't help himself. His analysis of the car was instinctive. Joseph was always fated to notice things other people did not.

'So what do you think I should do about it? Call the cops?' asked Selwyn accusingly.

'Maybe,' offered Joseph and Selwyn's face started to turn puce.

'Yeah, I'll get the cops down here. They'll fuck things up like they always do and, if I'm lucky, I'll never get a customer again. And if I ain't so lucky I'll end up in the foundations of that new recycling centre they're building. Go and get your cup of coffee, Joseph,' he snapped. 'Come back later.'

Joseph reprimanded himself for his stupidity as he walked out of Wray's garage. He should learn to keep his mouth shut. If people thought he was just a dumb old cab driver then that was just fine. It was safer that way, safer for him and safer for Yomi.

'Fucking cops,' he heard Selwyn mutter under his breath. 'Yeah, right,' Maybe he'd have two cups of coffee. First though, he would call in on Tony De Luca to see if he was interested in a little key-cutting job.

14

It was a long, cold walk to the parts yard and Joseph blew on his hands to warm them before he rapped on the locked office door. Somewhere from inside the yard a dog began to bark furiously and wouldn't let up. He waited a long while for a response but eventually a hard-faced man in his mid thirties peered out at him through the window.

Tony De Luca opened the door and frowned unhappily, as if he had just been rudely awakened from an afternoon nap. He looked Joseph up and down and said, 'Yeah?'

'Someone said you cut keys.'

'Someone was right,' he answered. 'But you could just go to a hardware store.'

'Yeah,' said Joseph. 'Can't do that. You see I ain't got no card for the keys, if you get me.'

'I get you.' De Luca nodded like he wasn't surprised. 'Then it's going to cost more, on account of the risk I'm taking doing it for you. Understand?'

'Of course.'

De Luca gave Joseph a price that would

apply to each key to be cut. It was way above the cost of having a normal set made but not so high it would put you off if you had a serious need for them, or a grievance with someone. Joseph agreed the price would not be a problem.

De Luca came out from behind his door and led him to a gate to one side of the office that was set into a long, wooden perimeter fence. He unlocked it with a key he pulled from an enormous set he was carrying that was clipped to his wide, leather belt. Tony De Luca was a big man with a large, pot belly, barrel chest and bare tattooed forearms all encased in a tight, white T-shirt that was covered in streaks of grease and engine oil. Despite the cold, he wore no coat.

The dog was still barking at Joseph as De Luca led him across the yard. It was a huge German Shepherd and it was straining at the leash to get at him. Some dogs just yap away all day and when they finally get set loose they think twice about going for the first man they see. Not this one. It was pulling on that chain leash like Joseph was its dinner and it hadn't eaten anything for days. Joseph wondered if it was true that dogs had a sixth sense about people, an intuition that meant they could tell when a guy came in off the street pretending to be someone he wasn't. They moved on past two lines of old cars that had been stripped and cannibalised for their working parts. Some had doors missing or a bonnet removed, others had wheels off or engine parts unceremoniously ripped from their guts. At the far end of the yard was a small warehouse with a wooden frontage and a little door cut into it that was secured by the biggest padlock Joseph had ever seen. Tony De Luca reached for his bundle of keys, found the right one, undid the padlock and opened the door, then they both stepped inside. They were now standing in a gloomy storeroom, where rack after rack of metal shelving stood side by side in rows, filled with seemingly endless, half-empty cardboard boxes, all labelled with their relevant auto parts. Joseph recognised a side panel for a Mustang sitting there on a shelf. De Luca had everything you might need, from windscreens to wheel nuts. There was probably enough in that storeroom to assemble several cars from scratch.

There was no conversation as they walked further into the warehouse, no 'where you from?' or 'you been busy?' De Luca was the kind of man who wanted to take your money and usher you out of his life with the minimum of complications, a guy who wouldn't understand the meaning of the phrase 'shooting the breeze'.

They reached a key-cutting machine that looked like it had been salvaged from the arc. It was much bigger than the one in the Williams' hardware store and unlike Merve's machine this one was covered in a layer of rust. It looked as if the only thing holding it together was the black grease that clogged its every surface.

'So, what you got?' asked De Luca.

'These,' Joseph held up the bunch of keys and De Luca blinked when he saw them, betraying something.

'You want one of each?' he said placidly.

'I guess, depends what you charging to do them all.'

'Yeah, well, there ain't no bulk discount,' he told Joseph firmly.

'Okay then,' Joseph smiled reasonably like it was no big deal.

De Luca put on a pair of plastic safety glasses and got to work on the first key. The machine made a series of harsh grinding noises and from time to time sparks flew as metal touched metal. De Luca spoke to Joseph without looking up from his work. 'I seen you around before?' he asked.

'Maybe,' answered Joseph. 'I drive a cab, so it's possible.'

There was no further conversation, but every time De Luca finished a key he would glance up at Joseph then quickly look away again, like he was trying to place him. Finally, when the work was finished, he handed Joseph the new bunch of keys, along with the old one. Joseph didn't move.

'There something else?' asked De Luca.

'Yeah,' said Joseph. 'You could tell me who else came in here recently with those same keys, asking for a new set. I know you recognise them. It was written all over your face.'

'I thought I recognised the key ring, that's all,' said De Luca. 'But there's got to be a million like it in New York, right?'

'I think a man who cuts signature keys illegally probably doesn't do that sort of work every day. I reckon he'd know if he'd worked on the same set twice in, say, a week or so.'

De Luca straightened, drawing himself up to his full height, his chest expanded like someone was pumping air into it and he clenched two fists the size of ham bones together meaningfully before taking a step towards Joseph. 'What are you? A cop?'

'No, but let's just say I got an interest in

knowing who else you've been doing business with lately. I just want the name, that's all.'

'Let's say something else,' and he took another step towards Joseph. 'How about I kick the living shit out of you right here and now then I drag your scrawny ass outside and let my dog finish the job in the yard for me while I watch with a cold beer in my hand. You like the sound of that, Mr Sticking-his-nose-in-where-it-don't-belong? Huh, do you?' and he jabbed a finger into Joseph's chest. It had the impact of a punch from a smaller man and Joseph rocked back on his heels.

'There's no need to get rough. I just want...'

'I heard what you want and you ain't getting it,' snarled De Luca. 'You ain't leaving here, neither, till I find out who you working for,' and with that he reached out a hand and plucked a solid metal wrench from the nearest work bench. He weighed it in his palm and advanced on Joseph. Oh, how he would have loved to have had Brigitte's gun in his hand right at that moment.

Joseph decided there and then that he had to make his move quickly, before De Luca had the opportunity to use the wrench or his massive fists first. He moved swiftly, propelling himself forwards on his toes and catching De Luca by surprise. As the bigger man tried to react by swinging the wrench at his head, Joseph ducked under the blow, aimed low and landed a heavy punch into De Luca's kidneys. He let out a breathless groan, the force of the blow enough to make the bigger man drop the wrench, which hit the ground with a high pitched clatter.

De Luca swore and Joseph followed straightaway with another venomous punch that crashed into the opposite side of the other man's torso hurting him in exactly the same spot. Joseph span De Luca round, grabbing his arm as he did so, propelling him forwards till he ran headfirst straight into the key cutter. Joseph slammed his head down until De Luca's cheek was pressed hard against the metal of the machine then he pulled De Luca's arm upwards, twisting it hard behind his back. He let out a cry of pain.

'Then quit struggling,' warned Joseph, twisting De Luca's arm once more for good measure.

Again he let out a cry, followed by a plaintive, 'Okay, okay.' Then, 'Let me go, man.'

'Not until you give me a name,'

'I don't know anything ... I ... argh!'

'Keep saying that and I'll keep on twisting your arm. You stay stubborn and we'll be here all afternoon, or at least until I lose interest and break it.'

'I don't take names,' cried the key cutter, sounding desperate now. 'I don't ask names and I don't take them. Did I ask you your name? I don't want to know your name and I didn't want to know his.'

'But you recognised the keys and you remember the guy, so what did he look like?'

'Okay, okay, don't do nothing,' pleaded De Luca. 'He was a big guy, stocky, you know, like he worked out a lot, talked to me like he was used to ordering guys around, had short cropped hair, looked like a grunt.'

'You saying he was a soldier?'

'Yes!' he said emphatically, then his tone softened. 'Maybe, hell, I don't know. Please let go of me.'

Joseph released his grip on the man's arm and De Luca flexed his injured limb gingerly before letting it hang limply across his chest like it was a wounded animal he was nursing back to health. Two minutes ago he'd been a tough guy, thought Joseph, now he looked like a kid who'd just had his lunch money stolen in the playground by the bigger boys.

'So you saying you thought this guy looked like he was a military type.'

'Yeah,' said De Luca, rubbing his arm miserably. 'Like I said, a grunt.'

Joseph had no desire to let De Luca go only to have the man set his dog onto him, so he left the parts dealer with two threats. 'Do anything to prevent me from leaving and I will break your arm, you got that?' The big man nodded meekly. It looked like all the fight had gone from him now. 'Then I'll go to the police, tell them all about your key-cutting business and show them the evidence.' He scooped up both sets of keys. 'And I'll suggest they take a good look at all those boxes of parts in here to see how many of 'em are stolen, you hear me?'

De Luca nodded, Joseph left the parts yard entirely unmolested. He strode calmly passed the German Shepherd, which predictably went crazy again, barking impotently at him as he walked by, tugging on its metal chain for all it was worth.

When Joseph returned Ardo's keys for the last time, he found the janitor in a contented mood. 'You know how the police keep questioning me abut the keys?' he asked rhetorically. 'The principal he pretty much tell them it's my fault. He say there are only three set of keys, one he has himself, one in the safe and one with the stupid janitor, who don't know where he puts them,' he said. 'Well it turns out I don't got to worry about that no more.'

'Why, what's happened?'

Ardo's eyes shone like he was about to let Joseph in on a big joke. 'Because they find another set of keys the principal don't know about.'

'There's a fourth set of keys?'

'Yeah,' he laughed. 'How you like that, Mr Smart-ass Principal fucking Geller?'

'Where'd they find them?'

Ardo chuckled. 'In the bushes.'

'The police found them?'

'They brought in a dog.' He laughed. 'Turns out it was a lot smarter than the cops. Whoever walked out of the building that night after killing Lopez must have panicked and thrown his keys as far as he could, but they didn't go far enough. One of the cops was searching the school grounds with that dog looking for clues and he found 'em. So now I can't get into no trouble, no more.' And his beaming smile showed his relief that suspicion had been lifted from his shoulders.

Joseph didn't want to put an end to his

friend's cheery mood but Ardo had clearly not considered the possibility that the keys in the bushes were merely a copy of the set he had left hanging on his nail in the boiler room. That was the obvious conclusion but he saw no point in ruining the janitor's day. It was more important right now to find out how the keys had come to be in the bushes that night. To discover that, Joseph would have to make one more visit.

15

Philip Ocher lived in a small, crumbling house in a bad part of town. It wasn't as rough out here as in the projects but it had to be a comedown for a former staff sergeant in the Marine Corps. Joseph waited at the door for a long while. He sensed someone was home but he knocked three times and received no answer. He was about to give up when the door was finally pulled back by a skinny, middle-aged woman who regarded him as if he might be a criminal come to ask her permission to rob the place, 'Whatever it is you're selling we ain't buying,' she said firmly in a southern drawl. This had to be Mrs Geller.

'I'm not selling anything,' assured Joseph and before she could say more, a shadow appeared behind her.

'It's all right, Lillian,' a deep, male voice said. 'It's one of the parents.'

'Stopping by the house?' she asked tetchily, before admitting Joseph with no words of welcome then going about her business.

'Please excuse my wife, she's tired.'

'I'm tired all right,' she said, like she was spoiling for a fight. 'Tired of this neighbourhood. These days when I open the door I never know who is going to be standing there.'

'Lillian, please,' pleaded Geller.

Joseph felt momentarily sorry for the coach as his wife walked away from him and up the stairs announcing firmly, 'I'm going to lie down.'

Joseph was ushered into a small sitting room, passing a solid wooden gun rack along the way. It was locked but there was enough space behind its doors to house assault rifles. Ocher was probably one of those survivalists, convinced the world is going to implode any day now and already planning for the moment when it happens. He likely had a cellar filled with tins of baked beans and a homemade water filtration system. Joseph began to wonder if the Soyinkas was the only home in the South Bronx that didn't have a gun in it.

Geller offered Joseph a seat. 'Please forgive Lillian. She's had it tough since we came here. It's not what she's used to. Some of the tours of duty I did, we had it pretty good.' Then he added proudly, 'Marine Corps looks after its own. I'll just be a moment,' and with that he left Joseph alone.

The room was sparsely furnished, one of the few personal touches were the photographs of Ocher's military career that adorned a small table in one corner. Geller saluting in full dress uniform, complete with the immaculate white-peaked cap and gloves of the United States Marine Corps, Geller on leave in some hot spot with Lillian, him in uniform and her in a cocktail dress, hanging off his arm like the dutiful wife, and finally Geller in civilian attire with his arms round a couple of army buddies in a bar – brothers in arms. Hung above the fireplace, dominating the room, was a large framed print of the famous Joe Rosenthal photograph of five Marine Corps men raising the Stars and Stripes on Mount Suribachi, high above the captured island of Iwo Jima. Joseph had seen a documentary on the History Channel about that decisive battle in World War Two, and he knew what that victory had cost. The route to that summit was strewn with the bodies of almost seven thousand U.S. Marines, which must have made its memory a particularly sacred and poignant one for men like Geller and his former comrades. The whole room was a shrine to the life this high school football coach once knew. Joseph got the impression he missed it all, badly.

When Geller returned he had two bottles of beer with him, their tops already removed. 'Thought we'd have a cold one.' He thrust out a muscular arm towards Joseph and handed him one of the bottles, then he said, 'Unless you ... er ... don't.'

'No, it's fine,' said Joseph. 'I have a beer from time to time.'

Geller looked relieved that he hadn't broken some religious or ethnic taboo and he released the bottle into Joseph's care then he sat down in the opposite armchair and took an enormous swig of his own beer. 'I guess you come to see me because of Yomi,' he said confidently as he wiped his mouth with the back of his hand. 'Mad at me, right?' There was a definite challenge in the tone, like he was proud to be the kind of guy who never shirked a confrontation.

'Mad at you?' asked Joseph, genuinely perplexed. 'Why would I be mad?'

'On account of how I switched him, from quarter back to running back.'

Joseph was dimly aware of the change in Yomi's football position but, in truth, it had hardly registered with him. The nuances of American football still eluded him for he had played what the Americans scathingly referred to as soccer when he was a boy. For his part, Joseph couldn't understand how a game that involved throwing a ball around and crashing into each other in padding could ever be described as football. In any case, his son had not exactly been devastated. If anything, Yomi seemed glad to be out of the spotlight. Joseph had certainly never dreamt of interfering with the coach's grand vision for the team.

'Quarter back got to be a leader,' continued Geller, 'and to tell you the truth I don't see that in your son right now. You'll forgive me if I'm blunt, it's just my way. Always has been.'

It was a statement not a question and Geller seemed inordinately proud of his own frankness. Joseph wasn't sure whether he would forgive Geller or not. He hadn't come here for a discussion about his son's shortcomings and he wasn't sure how much of a leader the boy was supposed to be at twelve.

'Go on,' he said.

'Boy's a follower right now, takes training too lightly to be a winner. I want to show Yomi he's got to earn his place in the team, has to fight for it, claw it back, got to want it bad, real bad. When he can show me that then maybe we'll have ourselves a quarter back.' Geller's eyes were shining like an evangelist now. He obviously thought he had just dangled the most tantalising carrot imaginable in front of Yomi's father.

To Joseph, this sounded like the kind of rhetoric he might expect to hear from a coach in the upper reaches of the NFL. Geller might think it was half time in the Super Bowl with everything to play for but Joseph was far from convinced. Instil that mentality into a young boy at his age and you were setting him up to feel like a failure when he was eventually told, as he inevit-ably would be, that he wasn't as good as the boy next to him. It might not happen for a few years, but it was bound to hit him all the harder when it did.

'To tell you the truth, Coach Geller,' said Joseph. 'I just want my boy to enjoy playing a little sport, that's all.'

'Nothing more than that?' asked Geller, not even trying to fake his disappointment. 'Football can give you a whole lot more than you think. Discipline, self sacrifice, team work...'

'What about fun?'

'Excuse me?' asked Geller, as if he was unfamiliar with the word.

'Fun. Enjoyment. Sportsmanship,' he added, before concluding with, 'learning to lose well.'

'Learning to lose?' Geller reacted as if Joseph had just added sodomy to the end of his list. 'Show me a good loser and I will show you a loser.'

'But not everybody can win, Coach Geller, so where does that leave us? With a nation of angry, frustrated, young men, all seething with resentment because they lost a football game? If they can't cope with that, then how are they supposed to manage if they lose their job, their girlfriend or don't finish top of the class every time they sit a test? How can they ever learn to succeed if they don't know how to fail? What happens to all the losers? Where do they go?'

'You're gonna think I'm being harsh,' said Geller confidently, 'but, years from now, they are the guys who'll be pumping your gas and flipping your burgers.'

The arrogance of the man was breath-taking. Joseph doubted if Geller considered driving a cab any nobler a profession than pumping gas. Yet here he was sitting in his crumbling house in a bad part of town, with a job in a low-ranked junior high school, acting like he was part of some Alpha male, upper echelon, charged with wheedling the weak and underachieving kids out of society. Men like Geller were dangerous, scarring kids, burdening them with unrealistic expect-ations then tossing them aside as soon as they failed to live up to some mythical standard most grown adults would struggle to attain. It would be laughable if it wasn't so serious.

'So if you're not mad at me for switching Yomi, then why exactly...' He didn't need to finish the sentence, the perplexed frown was enough.

'Am I here? I wanted to talk to you about Hernando Lopez.'

'Really?' asked the coach and there was a long pause while he waited for Joseph to ex-plain himself. 'I'm sorry, but I don't think I understand why you and I should be talking about that. Have I missed something here?'

'It's just like Principal Decker says, we all owe Mr Lopez. We owe him to think long and hard about what happened and to try and help the police investigation in any way we can. So I've been doing some of that long, hard thinking and I thought I'd better speak to you first before I talk to the police.'

'The police?' it wasn't Joseph's imagination. The coach's mouth was definitely dry. 'Why should this involve me?'

Joseph shrugged like it was no big deal. 'A couple of reasons. I keep hearing how you and he didn't get along.' Joseph was going out on a limb. It was purely a hunch on his part that the ex Marine and the liberal schoolteacher might not exactly share the same values. Conflict would have been likely and he was trying to draw Geller out.

'I had no beef with Lopez.' he spoke defensively but then softened. 'Okay, we didn't always see eye to eye but it don't mean I'd want to kill him! It's just he was a water-walker, if you know what I mean.'

'I don't think I do.'

'One of those guys who's always looking to give a bad apple a second chance, even when the rotten kid don't deserve it. When he took that knife off Jermaine, he should have marched that boy straight down to the principal and he would have been gone, out of there, no appeal. Instead he lets him off with a warning and ... well we all know what happened next.'

'You're saying Jermaine Letts murdered Mr Lopez,' countered Joseph. 'But no one believes that anymore, not even the cops. They let him go.'

'Excuse me? They had to let him go because there was insufficient evidence. Don't mean the little punk didn't do it and it don't mean the cops are happy about it neither. Let me tell you something about the world you and me live in, the real world. See that?' Geller pointed through the screen door at the rear of his house that overlooked the yard. An old Mercury was parked out back. 'I can't even keep it in the street no more, not if I want it to be there the next day.' He shook his head ruefully. 'Too many punk kids round here got too much time on their hands and no role models to look up to.'

'I guess the army would sort a lot of them out, would you say?'

'No,' said Geller to Joseph's surprise. 'I wouldn't say. Army's got to be professional. A country's armed forces got to be filled with people who want to be there. Good men, prepared to make the ultimate sacrifice so we can all sleep safe in our beds at night, not some juvenile offender sent there by a court, who starts bleating about how unfair it is when the bullets start flying. You think I want someone like that as my buddy, covering my lily-white ass when the shit hits the fan in Iraq or Afghanistan. If some raghead gets a bead on me, I want someone I can trust to take him down? No, sir. Army don't want 'em.'

'An interesting point, so what should we do with these young punks?'

'Put 'em to work. Make 'em clean the streets, repair the damage they caused, fix up their own shifty neighbourhoods. Like a chain gang only without the chain, I ain't an unreasonable man. But make it clear, say "son, it's either this or jail, so you got to get with the programme". I guess you think I'm old fashioned, well maybe I am. I believe in God, Unit, Corps and Country. I guess that makes me unfashionable these days.'

They had drifted from the topic of Hernando Lopez and it had been Geller who had carefully steered the conversation away from him. He was definitely hiding something, Joseph was sure of it. The coach had not seemed unduly aggrieved when Joseph had suggested that he and Lopez had been at loggerheads, even when he had made the link between that perceived conflict and a possible motive, however tenuous.

Joseph stayed silent for a while and waited for Geller to speak.

Eventually the coach said, 'So run it by me again, will you? You came down here because you heard Lopez and I banged heads from time to time and now you're going to tell the police you think I murdered him, that it?' He tried a forced laugh, as if the whole thing was absurd.

'That wasn't the only reason.'

'Well, let's see what else you got, shall we. Is it this?' He pointed to the print of Iwo Jima. 'Or this?' He waved a hand at the framed photos of army life. 'The guy was in the Marines, that's just got to make him a suspect. He's a trained killer after all.' He sneered at Joseph. 'That's like saying every man who steps in a boxing ring is likely to get in a fight outside a bar, but it don't happen and you know why? Discipline.' He shook his head. 'You know what really pisses me off?'

'No, but I've a feeling you're about to tell me.'

'Damn right, I am. People like you who

think the Marine Corps is the greatest thing on God's green earth when we are out there getting our asses shot off in some far-off hell hole, defending our country and your freedom. Yet the minute we're out of uniform, looking to make an honest living, you start acting like we're all wild animals who've been let loose in your neighbourhood,'

'It's not that.'

'Oh?' He was trying hard not to look concerned. 'What then?'

'The keys.' Joseph let the words hang in the air between them.

There was a long pause. Finally, the coach asked, 'What keys?' But his eyes told a different story.

'The keys for the school. You had a spare set cut down at De Luca's parts yard.'

The coach swallowed hard. He looked like he had just been punched in the guts. He opened his mouth to say something then closed it again. Eventually he managed to mutter the single word 'unbelievable', but Joseph wasn't going to let him off that lightly.

'I'm pretty sure those were the keys they found in the bushes and I reckon right now you're about as worried as can be that they're gonna find some usable prints on them, maybe even some DNA. If they can, then you know you're going to have some explaining to do.'

Once again, Coach Geller took a long time to answer. For a moment, Joseph thought he was going to demand his lawyer.

'What's the matter, Coach?' asked Joseph. 'You want to take the Fifth Amendment?' The question was intended to rile Geller and it worked.

'So I got some keys cut, so what?'

'You got some keys cut illegally. My guess is you lifted them while Ardo Piloyan was washing windows. You'd seen him do that often enough and you knew you'd have, what, half an hour, maybe even an hour. Is that why you asked Hernando Lopez to take football practice for you? It was, wasn't it? I don't know what you told him but it certainly wasn't the truth. So you went to the nearest place that'd do it without a card. I don't know how you knew that De Luca was running that kind of scam, maybe an old army buddy told you. Whatever, it doesn't matter. You then paid over the odds to get your own set of keys cut and you were back in time for Ardo to think they'd never even left the boiler room. The only question is, why you would go to so much trouble, risk losing your job, everything you got, just so you can let yourself in and out of the building when everyone else has gone home? I mean, it's not as if the football coach has to stay late and mark books now, is it? So why would you do that, Coach Geller?'

'I don't have to tell you nothing,'

'No you don't, you can tell it all to the police instead. I just wanted to see if you had a good explanation before I approached them, but I can see that you don't.' Joseph climbed to his feet and Geller bounced up after him, blocking his path to the door.

'Wait,' he said forcefully and Joseph braced himself for the attack that would surely follow. Was Geller really going to try and take him down in his living room while that highly strung wife was upstairs snoozing on their bed. 'I can't tell you why I needed the keys but you've got to believe me when I say I had nothing to do with Lopez dying. Jesus, the guy was okay. We didn't agree on everything, I thought he was too soft, sure I did, but I could see he had good intentions. Why in hell would I want him dead?'

'That's the bit I haven't figured out yet,' Joseph conceded. Then he shrugged. 'Maybe the police can.'

'No, wait a minute.' Geller grabbed Joseph's arm, gripping it tightly to try and prevent him from leaving. 'There's no need...'

'Let go of my arm,' said Joseph.

'Oh fuck,' said Geller, looking over Joseph's shoulder and out the front window. 'You called 'em.'

'No,' said Joseph turning in time to see five detectives climbing out of two un-marked cars that were now blocking Geller's driveway. 'I didn't,' but it was unmistakeably McCavity who was leading the way up Geller's path, her two favourite, burly officers in tow right behind her.

Geller sat back down in his chair and stayed there, ignoring the incessant ringing of the doorbell. Joseph didn't want to be the one to open the door to the police so he didn't move, either. Eventually, he heard the bad-tempered *thump-thump* of Mrs Geller's feet as she came down the stairs muttering to herself about how she had to do everything around here and never got a moment to herself. She didn't realise it just then but her day was about to get a whole lot worse.

As she answered the door, her voice drifted into the room and Joseph could hear the uncertainty in it. 'Yes?' she asked.

'Mrs Geller, I'm Assistant Chief McCavity of the NYPD.' The tone was brisk and businesslike. 'We'd like to speak to your husband.' And when Mrs Geller failed to answer, Joseph could easily imagine her standing there frozen and open mouthed on her own doorstep. 'If I may?' McCavity urged gently, and she must have reached out herself and opened the door wider then pushed in passed the shocked woman, for the next thing she was standing in the room, looking down at the ashen faced figure of the coach.

Philip Geller looked as if his world was about to come an abrupt end. He was still sitting there staring at the carpet when his wife followed McCavity into the room. 'Philip...' she began, but as soon as she saw him sitting there she knew something very bad indeed had happened. Any hopes that the police could've made some sort of mistake seemed to evaporate when she noticed the expression on her husband's face. For his part, Geller was trying not to look into her eyes.

McCavity said, 'We'd like to ask you a few questions, Mr Geller...' And it was then that she seemed to finally realise Joseph was sitting opposite the coach. 'What the hell are you doing here?' she asked and stared at him like she was dreaming and he couldn't be real.

'I had a few questions of my own,' he said.

'About a set of keys, by any chance?' she asked and Joseph nodded. 'Well what do you know?' she asked rhetorically then she transferred her attention back to the football coach.

Before she could say another word, the wife interrupted her. 'Philip, what's going on?'

'It's nothing, Lillian,' he said weakly, his face flushed. 'We'll talk about it later.'

'I'm afraid we've got to talk about it right now, Geller,' said McCavity. 'We need to know why your prints have been retrieved from a set of keys that was thrown in some bushes, a bunch of keys that you shouldn't have set eyes on.'

'It's not what you're thinking?' said Geller.

'Oh, really?' she asked. 'What *am* I thinking, Coach?' she said with mock good humour.

'That I had something to do with the killing of Hernando Lopez. That's what he, thinks, too.' He looked over at Joseph. 'But it ain't so, no way.'

'Then would you mind explaining to me why you had a spare set of keys for the school? Because you'd better have a very good reason.'

Geller looked like a man in a quandary. Joseph knew that even if he did have a good reason that was nothing to do with murdering a fellow teacher, his job, his livelihood, the new life Geller had built for himself at Antoinette Irving, limited as it was and so unappealing to his wife, was in jeopardy. At the very least, he had broken school rules and the law and he was likely to be dismissed from the school. These would be the concerns of an innocent man, but if he really was guilty of murder then they were the least of his worries.

Geller looked round the room at the expectant faces peering back at him and finally his eyes settled on his wife. She looked so confused, hurt and apprehensive. 'I can't tell you,' he said finally. 'I just needed 'em.'

'Very well,' said McCavity, 'in that case, Philip Geller, I'm arresting you for the murder of Hernando Lopez. You have the right to remain silent. Anything you say can and will be used against you in a court of law. You have the right to have an attorney present during questioning. If you cannot afford an attorney, one will be appointed for you. Do you understand?'

McCavity finished reading the coach his Miranda rights but her words were lost in the high-pitched shrieks of Geller's wife. She was crying, 'Philip, Philip, what's happening, what have you done, oh, Philip?' as he was hauled to his feet by the two burly and unsympathetic detectives.

Geller was handcuffed with his hands behind his back, then led to the door. It was only when the cuffs were actually on him that Philip Geller seemed to wake from his trance and realise the sheer magnitude of what was happening to him.

'You're making a mistake, please let me speak to you in private, my wife...'

'You can speak to me all you like down at the precinct, Mr Geller,'

'No, no, don't, you don't understand,' and the big man started to fight. He was trying to break free. The two detectives were also heavy-set men and Geller was in handcuffs but they were struggling to hold onto the big man as he tried to prevent their progress towards his front door. 'No, hear me out, it's not what you think, I didn't kill anyone.' He was shouting now, kicking out at the two men and trying to use his feet to stop them from dragging him along, wedging them into door frames and pressing back against them. 'This whole thing, it's not about Lopez, it's about a girl, just a girl, god damn it.' Then he let out a stifled moan as one of the two detectives tired of the fight and landed a crafty, unseen blow into his torso to cease his struggles.

Joseph didn't know who was the more stunned by the clean-Marine's admission, Geller's wife or himself

'Philip?' she said in a high-pitched, panicked voice, as her husband was bundled through the door and into the police car. She kept repeating, 'Philip, Philip? What have you done?'

But Geller was saying nothing. His shocked, red face simply stared out of the car window, as if his wife wasn't there at all. The car pulled away, leaving Lillian Geller plaintively calling his name over and over as it disappeared with her husband.

'Take her in our car,' ordered McCavity. 'We'll need to speak to her, too.' And poor, dumbstruck Mrs Geller was led away as well.

McCavity paused on the driveway for a moment to speak to Joseph. She did not seem pleased with him. 'Well, we do keep bumping into each other, don't we? People will start to talk,' she said. 'Always one step ahead of the dumb old NYPD, aren't we, Mr Solinka? It's amazing really, the resources I got at my disposal; all those detectives out there working their butts off for me twenty-four-seven, forensic teams in their little laboratories testing keys and knives for prints and DNA and yet, when we finally turn up at the killer's house, here you are already. There's just one thing I don't get. We're here because one of my hard-working guys found some keys in a bush that shouldn't have been there or any place else. Another took a witness statement from a pupil who saw Coach Geller with his own set of keys for the school. When my officer learned that he shouldn't have his own set we knew we had our man. Once the prints we took off the keys from the bushes matched the ones Geller had on file, this was sewn up. But you couldn't possibly have known what my detective was told. So what are you doing down here?'

'You're forgetting I used to be a detective myself back in...'

'Back in Lagos, yah-huh, I forget nothing, Mr Solinka.' Except my name he thought. 'Sherlock Holmes couldn't have known that Coach Geller's keys were in that bush.'

'No, but I spoke to a man in a parts yard right by the school who admitted he cut a set of keys just like those very recently. He then described a man who sounded almost exactly like Philip Geller.'

McCavity's mouth opened and she seemed

a little lost for words. 'Holy ... and just how did you get him to do that?'

'I coaxed it out of him.'

'You coaxed it out of him.' She snorted a bitter and humourless little laugh. 'And who might this cooperative man be?'

Joseph owed no loyalty to Tony De Luca and he knew that withholding evidence would put him in a lot of trouble with McCavity. She looked like she needed very little reason to throw the book at him right now, so he gave her the man's name without protest.

McCavity nodded. 'And you'd have given me that name when exactly?'

'Right after I'd been to see Geller for his explanation. Didn't want to bother you till then. I guess this time you were one step ahead of me.'

'Don't patronise me, Mr Solinka, I don't appreciate it.' She turned to one of her detectives and gave him De Luca's name and address then ordered, 'Bring him in for questioning, right now.' Then she turned back to Joseph. 'This better stack up,' she told him, not needing to add an 'or else'.

The message was clear. McCavity had spelt it out for him in fact. She didn't like her modern, high-tech, scientific police force being made to look second rate by a lone, amateur sleuth, who had learned his skills in some third-world backwater. Joseph had made himself too high profile for McCavity's liking. He could tell that any chance she got from now on, she was likely to make his life difficult.

16

'I never trusted Philip Geller,' said Brigitte firmly. 'And I'm not just being wise after the event.'

'Female intuition, or did he give you cause to think he was a murderer?' asked Joseph as he steered the cab round a tight corner on the way to her apartment.

'It's not that,' said Brigitte. 'I'm not claiming he was my first pick as a murder suspect. I'm just saying there was something about him that was hard to like. He always struck me as being wired way too tight, like if there was one man I'd have guessed might one day show up at Antoinette Irving with an M-16 and go postal, it was him.' Joseph laughed. 'What?' she asked.

'You,' he said. 'I take you to a shooting gallery a couple of times and you already know your M-16s from your Uzis, then you say that some other guy looks like he might enjoy loosing off a few rounds in public. Seriously though, you've got to be careful. Make sure you're not trying to fit a guy to a crime just because you don't like him. Geller could be the biggest neo-con, clean-Marine, George Bush loving, flag saluting, bible basher in the city, but that don't necessarily make him a murderer.'

'I didn't say it did,' she argued, 'and how do you know I'm not a flag-flying neo-con myself? What makes you think I'm not a George Bush lover with a picture of Dick Cheney on my mantelpiece and an 'I Love Donald Rumsfeld' T-shirt on underneath my Antoinette Irving sweatshirt? How can you be so sure you know what makes me tick?'

'Apart from the fact you have a brain? Let's see; the way you dress, the newspapers and magazines you read, the fact that you care about the kids in your school and have actually left America and seen some other countries. You know that there is a whole, complicated world out there and I don't think seeing that would turn you into a card-carrying Republican.'

238

'Mmm, well.' She seemed a little put out. 'Some of that may be true, Joseph, but don't go thinking you know me completely, based on the clothes I wear and the magazines I read. Life isn't always that simple, Mr Ace Detective. There's plenty of people out there that would make unkind assumptions about you, but it doesn't make them true.'

'I guess they would.' Joseph knew what she meant and he was a little annoyed with her now, like she was saying it's okay that you're a cab driver from one of the world's most corrupt countries, I can see through that but there are many who wouldn't. He wasn't sure why, but her words stung him a little.

Perhaps it was this that made him continue the argument about the coach. 'I'm just saying that Geller having a spare set of keys doesn't necessarily make him a murderer.'

'Even though you said as much yourself? You asked me if it was possible to get a spare set of keys cut for precisely that reason.'

'Yes, and you told me it was impossible, if you recall. That was another conclusion you jumped to.'

'Are you pissed at me, Joseph?'

'No.'

'You are, aren't you? Is it because I had an opinion on the case? Am I not entitled to have one? I may be an amateur but surely ... or is it because I'm a woman? Don't they have any female detectives in Lagos?'

Joseph didn't know how to answer that one. He didn't give a damn about her being a woman but he had to admit she was right. He *was* pissed at her. He was irritated by her unblinking assumption that Philip Geller was a murderer, for little more reason than she disagreed with his politics and his ethos on life was alien to her. Joseph had always seen Brigitte as a died-in-the-wool liberal, she was a Bill Clinton fan, who freely admitted she thought it was little more than mildly amusing that the president got a blow job from an intern in the oval office, just as long as he was still benignly watching over the country, keeping it safe from the right-wing military industrial complex. She had deplored the tales of Guantanamo Bay and the 'extraordinary rendition' of terrorist suspects to Camp X-Ray, calling it 'little more than legalised kidnapping with no right of trial or appeal'. How ironic then that she should be so quick to judge someone on such little evidence. If a Republican had been convinced a hippy type was a murderer just because he wore a beard and had burned his draft card during Vietnam she would have been up in arms. Now, when it suited her, Brigitte's own political bias was enough for her to condemn Geller. It was as unscientific as putting him in the frame for murder because his eyebrows met in the middle.

Perhaps he was being too harsh. He told himself it was not Brigitte's fault if she took an instinctive view of these things. She might not be as thorough and reserved as a seasoned detective but he realised she was probably entitled to her prejudiced view-point on the man, just like everybody else. Besides, wasn't Geller always so quick to condemn the youngsters in his care?

'I'm sorry, I didn't mean it to sound like that. It's just I've been bothered about it ever since I left Geller's house. I arrived there thinking maybe he'd done it but I left there convinced that he hadn't.' She opened her mouth to speak and he interrupted her. 'I know, I know, I'm using the same intuition as you, only my gut feeling is going the other way. Again, I have to ask what is the guy's motive? He and Lopez didn't get along, so what? You and Geller don't get along, either, but I don't see you taking pot shots at him in the school car park. It just doesn't stack up. Then there was that thing he said about a girl when he was being led away. He left it right up till the end, like it was costing him a lot to say it.'

'Well his wife was there, wasn't she?'

'Which made me think it might be true.'

'Mmm.'

'What?'

'Well, there was talk, rumours I suppose you could say about Geller and some of the girls.'

'What kind of talk?'

'That he wasn't exactly proper in the way he handled himself around them.'

'In what way?'

'You want details? I don't know. It was just a vibe I picked up from some of them and from a couple of the other teachers. It was the way he carried himself when he was around them, something intangible, inappropriate touching, that sort of thing. I don't mean he went up to them, grabbed their breasts and went 'honk!', I just heard that he was a little...'

'Less than politically correct.'

'Yeah,' she agreed, 'and he'd make comments of the "my how you have grown, young Amy Carter" variety. Not something you could report him for because it could all be dismissed as innocent. He'd say stuff to them that he could claim was just about them having grown taller since last semester but really he was talking about them being well built. I mean that's not nice for a thirteen- or fourteen-year-old girl to have to hear from a teacher.'

'No,' he agreed. 'You're right. It isn't.'

'A man like Geller,' she continued, 'spends his whole time with men, except for the wife he's probably known since they first dated back in high school. I don't think he gets women. I don't reckon he understands them. It's that Madonna-whore thing some men have, you know. They think women are all either virgins they can bring home to mom then marry, or sluts who'll lay down for anybody, when the truth is a little more complex.'

'Is it?'

'Now I know you are teasing me, Joseph, so stop it. You know it is.' She smiled. 'I may not know everything about everybody but I am sure of this one, small thing, you are no Philip Geller. You understand women, Joseph, I know you do.'

She was right, to a degree. He had known women, a number of them, right up until he met Apara and had convinced himself that he would never look at another. And then Apara had died and suddenly he was back out there in the big world, alone again.

Brigitte pulled down the sun visor and took a moment to examine her reflection in the mirror. When she was happy with the state of her hair and make-up, she pushed the visor back into place. 'Soon be home,' she said a little self-consciously. 'You got time for coffee?'

The cab had never really warmed up during the short journey back to Brigitte's apartment and the atmosphere had become a damn sight colder once Joseph politely declined her invitation for coffee. The look on her face had said it all. Before he was given the chance to explain that he had things to do, before he could begin to intimate that he wasn't sure coffee was such a good idea, particularly when he was pretty damn sure she didn't mean just coffee, she had thanked him for the shooting lesson and climbed out of the cab.

'Are you okay?' he asked, immediately realising he'd somehow messed up.

'I'm fine,' she said primly then walked off before he could respond, leaving Joseph to drive back to the project alone.

So Brigitte was mad at him, in a way that all women were mad at all men from time to time. Not really mad, not pan-throwing, crockery-smashing, stab-you-through-the-heart-with-a-carving-knife mad. No, Brigitte was the kind of mad where if he bothered to ask her whether she was mad she would simply and calmly say 'no', even when the correct answer was yes. If he was then foolish enough to ask her if she was okay she would reply 'fine'. Joseph had been married for almost fifteen years and he knew what 'fine' meant. To a man it meant okay, maybe even great, as in a fine wine. To a women it meant I am mightily pissed off and about to declare war on you. When Apara said, usually through gritted teeth, that she was 'fine' he knew she was about to go to Def con Two and he was in big trouble. At that point he would usually go away and sit somewhere quietly until he could attempt to work out her reasons for being pissed at him. Then, whether he felt she was being entirely reasonable or not, he would try to find some way to thaw the ice that had magically appeared between them.

Was that what he was supposed to do to Brigitte? He didn't think so. In fact, he was a little annoyed at her himself for he had never promised her anything more than friendship. Sure there had been some harmless flirting and they spent time together outside of school hours but he had never even asked her out on a date the shooting gallery didn't count, nor did coffee afterwards in the crumbling diner. Now apparently she felt hurt and rejected. Since when did it become bad manners to not sleep with a woman, damn it?

'Always open doors for a lady,' his father had counselled him when he was a boy. 'Pull out her chair when she wants to sit at the table and stand up when she wishes to leave the room,' he had added gravely. His father was big on old-school manners but he had never once said to Joseph, 'And above all make sure you go to bed with them whenever they want, or you might hurt their feelings!'

So what was he supposed to do now? Drive back over there, knock on her door and apologise or belatedly climb into bed with Brigitte and run the risk of hurting her further when things didn't work out, as was entirely likely?

In truth, he couldn't see beyond his current situation right now. Even allowing for the crummy job and apartment, the knife-carrying son, the seriously injured friend and the unsolved murder that Yomi was caught up in, he had enough to contend with, without attempting a relationship as well. Brigitte De Moyne was probably cursing him right now but what could he do about it? Everyone has their problems.

17

There was no moon, so Joseph parked his cab in a blind spot by the wreckage of a burned-out garage. From here he could not be seen but he could easily make out the row of vandalised lockups Eddie had been staking out when he was beaten senseless. It was a bitterly cold night and Joseph was unable to leave the cab's engine running so instead he had taken a thick, woollen blanket from his apartment and wrapped it round himself. It was nowhere near sufficient. After more than two hours, Joseph could no longer feel his feet and he had grown tired of watching his breath come out before him in little white clouds that misted up the windscreen of the Crown Victoria.

He had put his phone on silent setting and the little screen suddenly lit up on the dashboard with an incoming call. It was Cyrus, phoning yet again to see if Joseph had decided to talk to his manager about the concierge job. Joseph turned off his phone.

This was the third night he had put aside some precious hours to watch the lockups and there had been no sign of the Crips' Killers or anyone else. He was about to give up for the night and maybe for ever when an ancient pick-up truck rattled round the corner. As it drew nearer, Joseph could see that there were boxes of stolen electrical items tied down on the flat bed with lengths of rope, only partially covered with a greasy length of tarpaulin. The gang didn't seem to care too much if anyone saw them or their precious cargo.

When the vehicle drew to a halt, the doors of the double-cab van opened and out stepped a small gang of tough-looking girls, though that seemed an inappropriate word to describe these youthful gangsters. They all had a wild and wired look and there was precious little about them that was feminine in Joseph's eyes. Probably high on something, he thought, to give them the courage to go ahead with their heists. Joseph understood how this kind of operation might work. All it needed was someone on the inside. Some low-paid worker who could keep his or her eye open down at a warehouse or the dockside and supply a tip-off when a suitably heavy-laden lorry or container was coming in. Then either someone was paid off and a small percentage of a large haul was ripped off, or the gang could use force and take the lot. Joseph suspected it would be more likely that this gang would have a contact in a low-key security position, someone who could leave doors open or steal keys for copying down at a yard like De Luca's.

They had trained the headlights of the truck on one of the few lockups that still had a working door on it. This way they could see what they were doing as they began to unload their bounty. It allowed Joseph to watch them closely in the beams. There were five girls dressed in a similar street style, all leather jackets, blue-and-white bandanas and a couple of baseball caps turned back to front. They moved quickly, efficiently, like they'd done this often enough before and knew what they were doing. Joseph counted the boxes and it seemed like a pretty good haul. The large, flat cardboard ones looked like plasma TV sets and the smaller, heavier loads that took longer to offload had to be computers. Joseph wondered casually who they were ripping off to get all this stuff, but that wasn't why he was here. He waited until they had almost completed their task then he calmly climbed out of the car and strode right up to the gang.

Joseph stepped from the shadows and said softly, 'I'm looking for Rihanna Letts.'

They all started and one of them cried, 'Motherfucker!' like he had almost given her a heart attack.

'She ain't here,' said the girl who had recovered the quickest, the one who seemed to carry the most authority in the group. By the way she spoke up, with no fear of contradiction, Joseph assumed she was the leader. He also recognised her face. She had been the swaggering, hip-rolling little madam, who had told the assembled parents and teachers of Antoinette Irving, 'We done with you.'

'You need to get a new line, Rihanna,' said Joseph. 'Your momma's already worn that one out.'

'Who the fuck are you?' she challenged him.

The other girls adopted threatening poses like they were all set to rush this stranger who was threatening their leader.

'Just a guy with some questions,' he said.

'About what?'

''Bout an old man who got his head busted open right here on this very spot by a bunch of gals around your age.'

Rihanna laughed. 'He told you then.' And she sneered. 'Didn't think he would ever tell nobody 'bout that – too shamed. I bet that interfering piece of shit wasn't expecting to get his white ass bitch-slapped like that when he came down here. You looking for the same treatment?'

'No I'm just looking for some answers.' The girls were all watching him intently, waiting on a cue from their leader. 'I want to know why Macy Williams wasn't with you that night, the night you put my friend Eddie in hospital.'

'Mr, have you got a gun?' she asked incredulously. 'You must have, you come down here talking to me like that. I ain't got to tell you shit. You've got some balls, on our turf, 'dissing us like this.'

'This ain't your turf, Rihanna, I live here, so do a lot of other people and they are getting tired of you, your friends and all of your bullshit. Eddie tried to tell you that but you didn't get the message. I'm telling you the same thing. Close your operation in this pro-ject before someone shuts it down for you.'

'You?' she sneered. 'No way.'

'I won't need to, believe me and that ain't even why I'm here.'

'Then why are you here?'

'I just want to know about Macy Williams and why she isn't in your gang no more.'

'Fuck you,' she told him. 'I don't answer no questions from no one. Cops can't make me, you sure as hell won't make me.' She was trying real hard to be tough, which was bad news for Joseph because it made her a dangerous person, a leader with a point to prove. 'Maybe we should give you some of what your friend got,' she said menacingly and she started to move towards him then. 'You want to wake up in the hospital? You want us to stomp your motherfuckin' head all over here, huh?'

They were all moving towards him now.

Joseph had never struck a woman before. He would never even have considered himself capable of such an act until now but it seemed, as the girls started to walk forward, forming a menacing semicircle around him that they might not leave him with a choice. Hands were delving into pockets, reaching for hidden weapons. He had to assume there would be knives, homemade coshes, clumsily fashioned knuckle-dusters, the usual paraphernalia of the small-time street gang. They looked like they were a close-knit group, who would fight ferociously for each other, more like young men than girls and he would have to treat them accordingly if he didn't want to end up like Eddie. Joseph stood straight, tall and unmoving, he puffed out his chest and bunched his hands into fists so they could see them.

'Just one thing you gotta remember before you start something with me,' he said it quietly, very calmly. 'I'm no old man,' and he looked her straight in the eye.

Rihanna hesitated, for just a second but it was long enough for Joseph to see the doubt in her eyes. The question was, would she back down in front of her crew?

'You the guy who called on my momma, ain't ya?'

'That's right.'

'Upset my kid brother.' Joseph shrugged like it was of no consequence. It didn't do to show weakness in front of these people. 'Said you believed him in the end, though.' Joseph nodded. 'Must be the only one thinks he didn't kill that teacher.'

'Maybe at first, but the police believe it now. Surprised you ain't heard, they took Coach Geller into custody, looking to pin Lopez's death on him.'

'No!' She said it with glee. 'You shitting me, right?' Joseph shook his head. 'Was it 'cos you said something to them about him?' Joseph would never normally have taken any credit for that but he realised what she was doing. She was giving herself an out, a reason not to try and take him. Rihanna Letts wasn't sure she could beat Joseph in a fight and now she needed an excuse to avoid starting one.

'I came to the same conclusion the police did, around the same time,' he said non-committally.

'Then it looks like my brother owes you,' and the gang visibly relaxed around him, stepping down from their collective sense of high alert. 'But what's this shit about Macy? What do you care she ain't in our crew no more?'

'Guess you fell out over a boy, huh?'

'A boy?' She laughed at that and the rest of the gang laughed with her. 'No, weren't no boy, Mr. Macy is into men, not boys. She likes men so much we don't never see her no more. There was no fight. I didn't kick her out of the crew, she did that herself, she's just not around these days.'

'So that's why you took your little brother out with you.' And that was all he really needed to know.

'Where you going?' she asked, as if they

had unfinished business to discuss, but he had already turned and was walking back to his cab.

'Just you make sure you take my advice, Rihanna,' he called back over his shoulder. 'Quit using these lockups.'

'Fuck you, you motherfucker!' she screamed after him. ''Crips' Killers gonna git you, you ever come round here again! You going down, you hear!' But Joseph wasn't listening. He climbed into the cab and got the hell out of there.

As he drove, his mind went back to the day when he had stood on the line with Brigitte at the football practice, watching Yomi being put through his paces by Coach Geller. Macy Williams had driven by then, tooting the horn of her silver Honda Accord, windows rolled down, and waving like a diva, all blonde hair and attitude. She was making sure everybody could see her, like she was trying to impress somebody. At the time he'd assumed it must have been a boy whose head she was attempting to turn, but it had puzzled him, as the oldest one on the pitch had to be fourteen and she was a good three years older than that. Macy Williams was practically a woman. It was only when Rihanna Lefts had said 'Macy is into men not boys' that it all fell into place and, in that same instance, Joseph finally knew who had killed Hernando Lopez.

18

What was it Marjorie said was the cause of most normal, average, everyday murders? Money and fucking, that's what. Joseph was about to put that notion to the test.

The apartment block was quiet when he pulled up outside. It was another cold, late evening and all but the most daring or foolish were safely at home by now, waiting for Letterman. At least he would be indoors tonight, after three cold spells in his car down by the lockups. Joseph had staked out the Crips' Killers and warned them off. Predictably they hadn't listened. His time there had been more than worth it though. Rihanna Letts didn't know it but her words last night had just blown the lid off the Hernando Lopez case and she had left Joseph cursing that he had not spotted it sooner.

He parked his cab in a tiny space, right next to a shiny new Honda Accord in front of a big, yellow van with the name of an energy company stencilled on it, then he walked up to the main door of the building. Merve Williams' family had a good-sized apartment in the Port Morris Clock Tower, an imposing, five-storey, red-brick building that dominated its surroundings. The Bloomberg administration had famously eased New York's planning restrictions and the tower was one of many old warehouse buildings eagerly bastardised by developers. Now the area known as the Gateway to the Bronx was filling up with wannabe yuppies and local families on the up, like the Williams clan.

Merve seemed pretty surprised to hear Joseph's voice on the intercom. 'Joseph? It's a little late.'

'It's important, Merve. I need to speak to you. It's about Macy.'

There was no response from Merve. The silence had Joseph wondering if the hardware-store owner had decided he didn't need to speak to anyone at this hour. Perhaps he left him hanging on the doorstep talking to himself. Just as Joseph was about to speak again, he heard the loud, jarring buzz of the automated door, followed by a heavy click as it sprang open to permit him entry.

The building was new enough to trust the

lift and Joseph was greeted by the man himself standing at his front door, which he held open a little reluctantly to admit his unexpected guest. Joseph followed Merve into a small study. The desk light and laptop were already on, so it looked like Merve was working late, balancing his books.

'As you can see, I'm a little busy right now,' he said hesitantly,

'This won't take long. Anyone else in?'

'My wife's taken Laura and her brother to see some movie. Macy's out.' He attempted a rueful smile. 'She's never in, you know kids.' Then he seemed to remember Joseph was an uninvited guest.

'What's this about?' Merve was grim faced as he sat behind his desk. 'You said it was something to do with Macy?' He was trying to look surprised.

'Well, partly.'

'Either it is or it isn't, Joseph,' answered Merve irritably.

'Like I say, Merve, it's partly about Macy and partly about someone else.'

'I don't think I understand.'

'The part about Macy involves her seeing someone she shouldn't have been seeing, someone in a position of authority who should have known better than to spend his time chasing after a seventeen-year-old girl.'

Merve listened to Joseph intently, but his face was a mask. He was giving nothing away. 'Now, are you going to tell me that Macy wasn't seeing one of her teachers, Merve?' Merve straightened, but he did not contradict Joseph. 'And are you then going to deny you recently found out about it?'

'I don't know who you've been listening to, Joseph, and I can't imagine why you'd believe every bit of malicious gossip you hear.'

'Oh, I talk to a lot of people but this isn't just gossip.'

Merve seemed to make a decision then. 'I haven't got time for this,' he said and started to rise from his chair. Evidently he was about to ask Joseph to leave.

'Fine, I guess I'll just have to go and talk to Assistant Chief McCavity down at the precinct instead. She always has time to talk, particularly when it's about a murder case she's working on.'

'Murder?' Merve said the word scornfully but he sat right back down. 'We both know Macy had nothing to do with that school teacher getting stabbed.'

'Oh, yes she did,' said Joseph firmly. 'She had everything to do with it.'

'Now just you wait a minute...'

'No, you wait,' interrupted Joseph. 'Do you want to hear me out? That way you'll know everything I know. Or do you want to wait till the cops and the lawyers are involved and you are trying to second-guess them all? Do you really want to run that risk or would you rather hear all about how your daughter got mixed up in a murder? Do you want to know what I've got?'

Merve snorted. 'You just go ahead with your half-assed theories, Joseph. I ain't stopping you.' And he folded his arms defiantly across his chest.

'I should have noticed sooner, at the football practice when they arrested Jermaine Letts. You were there with Laura watching her brother and you had your car with you, so they didn't need a ride from their big sister. But along came Macy anyhow, in that hatchback you gave her, sounding the horn and waving so that everybody could see her. I remember thinking at the time she must have been showing off like that to catch the eye of some boy, but they were all younger than her, so why would she want to be there? Unless it wasn't a boy whose eye she was looking to catch.'

'Just what are you accusing my daughter of?'

'An affair,' said Joseph simply. 'It's a strange, old-fashioned word these days and it isn't illegal, not in this country at any rate, but I guess that's what you would call it. It's an affair if she's having a relationship with a married man, isn't it? I mean, what would you call it, Merve?'

Merve stayed silent. Instead he opened up his desk draw and put a hand in, and for a second Joseph thought he might actually be reaching for a gun. Instead, he brought out a pack of cigarettes and an old, silver lighter. He lit himself a cigarette and sat back like he was waiting for the story to continue. Joseph didn't disappoint him. 'Coach Geller admitted to the police that he had a spare set of keys for the school. He shouldn't have had them and he wasn't too keen to own up to it, until they accused him of the murder of Hernando Lopez. Finally, he told them he had the keys because of a girl. Not a woman, I remember, but a girl. You would have expected a man of his age to use a more mature word to describe someone he might be having a secret affair with. That is unless the man in question is a teacher and we are talking about a former pupil, who is still only seventeen, then of course 'girl' would be the right word.'

Merve's eyes narrowed at the suggestion

but, crucially, he didn't contradict it. Joseph continued. 'Do you think the cops are dumb? They're gonna ask him who he's been seeing and he's going to tell them eventually. It's the only way he can wriggle out of a murder charge. Let's agree that the coach abused his position in order to take up with an ex-pupil he met through her younger brother, shall we? My guess is Macy met the coach when she was dropping off her brother at a game, or maybe she drove by one night when he was taking practice, she waited behind to speak to him and they ended up together, your Macy and the married guy.'

'Watch your mouth, Joseph,' cautioned Merve. 'That's my daughter you're talking about.'

Joseph carried on regardless. 'Or maybe he approached her while she was watching her brother going through his paces and the coach was walking the touchline. Who knows how it panned out but either way the end result was the same, they began a relationship.' Joseph had chosen the last word carefully. He wanted Merve to stay calm, for now.

'One of Geller's colleagues told me he had an eye for the ladies and there is always one young, vulnerable girl in any school who might think a guy in a position of authority, a man who used to wear a uniform, who fought for his country, was an attractive proposition. She isn't the first to look longingly at a teacher and she won't be the last.'

'I'm warning you...'

Joseph nodded calmly. 'That's very decent of you, Merve. What are you going to do? Stab me? Huh?' Merve Williams looked visibly shaken, like his whole world just came crashing down around him. 'Is that what you're planning to do? Just like you stabbed poor, innocent Hernando Lopez?'

Merve was shaking his head repeatedly from side to side. He looked like he was trying to convince himself as much as Joseph. 'I didn't.'

'Sure you did. The only thing I don't know is whether you actually thought your daughter was sleeping with Lopez or you came gunning for Geller and the wrong man disturbed you. I can see you are a little upset right now, Merve, so I'll just carry on telling you what happened then you can correct me if I get any of it wrong.'

'Jesus Christ,' said Merve weakly. He had his head in his hands now.

'Like I said, Macy was seeing Coach Geller, for whatever reason,' Joseph would never know that reason for sure but he wondered if it might not have a little to do with rebelling against an over-controlling father. Or maybe it was a whole lot simpler than that. Joseph knew a little something about human nature after so many years as a detective and some things were the same in Highbridge as they were in Lagos. Did it make Macy feel extra naughty to be felt up in the back seat of Geller's car, knowing his unquestioning wife was waiting at home for him? Did she get an extra kick out of sex with the guy sensing her father would be so ashamed of her if he knew the truth? For some people it isn't exciting unless it's a secret, it isn't fun unless it's forbidden and it isn't good unless it's very bad indeed.

'Of course, I don't know how you found out but you can explain that to the police yourself. You obviously suspected she was up to something a little more serious than dating a boy her own age.' When Merve looked up again, his face was streaked with tears. 'Then you found the keys to the school right here in your house and you knew there was no way Macy should have them. You worked out what was going on right there and then, didn't you Merve? Macy got those keys from her older, married lover. She was meeting him down at the school when everybody else had gone home. Maybe they got tired of his car. They couldn't exactly go back to his place, or yours, could they? A motel wouldn't do, either, in case the staff got suspicious about her age.'

'Joseph, please...' He was pleading because he didn't want to hear the details. It was amazing, thought Joseph, a man has died because this stupid girl took her clothes off then opened her legs for some brainless teacher having a mid-life crisis, but Merve still couldn't bear to think about his precious daughter rolling around with an older guy.

'So you took that set of keys from Macy and you went looking for the man who seduced your daughter. She was seventeen, just seventeen, and he was using her, wasn't he, Merve? You went there with just one idea in your head. You were going to get hold of that guy and you were going to make him pay for what he'd done.'

'No.'

'Oh yes. Why else would you go down there when everybody else had gone home? You didn't report it to the principal or the police and you *did* go down there. Do you know how easy that will be to prove? You never go inside that building, Merve. Football practice is the only thing I've ever seen you at. It's their momma who's on the PTA. She's the one goes to the parents' evenings and you weren't at the principal's meeting, but I'll be willing to bet your DNA is all over that corridor. It's not like the old days, they can find fibres, tiny drops of sweat and blood. Lopez's blood was everywhere so his DNA's going to be on your clothes in your car. Did you try and clean your car, Merve?'

'Fuck you,' snarled Merve and Joseph knew the realisation was dawning on him. He was trapped.

'So what happened, Merve? You went into the school and there was nobody there except this one little guy – a maths teacher marking books, probably setting out the homework for the next day's schooling. Luckless Hernando Lopez, his only crime was to be a hard-working teacher. He was probably walking out of there after a long day and he bumped right into you, an enraged father. Is that how it went? Did you accuse him outright of screwing your daughter?'

'Shut up.'

'I'm not going to shut up, Merve and you can't go on pretending this didn't happen,' said Joseph. 'Is that how it played out? Only he probably got real scared, when this big, heavy-set guy who just wouldn't listen to reason suddenly started to push him around. Well, you would be scared, alone in the dark like that with a strange man threatening to smash you to a pulp. I guess that's why he made his big mistake. Lopez remembered he still had Jermaine Letts' knife in his pocket, so he pulled it out and waved it around a little, didn't he, shouted at you to get back too I should imagine. Only you didn't step back, did you, Merve? You went right up to Lopez, snatched that knife out of his hand like you were taking a popsicle from a baby then stabbed him with it.'

'No way.'

'Wasn't that how it was? What was it like then, Merve? Are you going to tell me you didn't enjoy killing him, the guy you believed defiled your daughter? Sure you did.'

Joseph was trying to goad Merve Williams into a reaction and he succeeded. 'Stop it! Stop it!'

Merve was breathing hard as he got to his feet and stumbled over to the cabinets that were set against the far wall of his office. 'How many people have you told this crock of shit to Joseph?' he asked. 'You ain't been to the police yet, else they'd have been here,' He opened the largest wooden door to reveal the safe behind it and began quickly

267

turning its dials. Surely he wasn't dumb enough to take the cash and run for it. How far did he think he would get with everybody looking for him? 'My guess is you ain't told nobody yet.' And with that he turned back from the open safe and Joseph realised that Merve Williams was holding a gun.

'Don't point that thing at me, Merve, it might go off.'

'Maybe that's what I was intending.'

'You're planning to shoot me in your own home?' asked Joseph calmly. 'That'd be smart, real smart. I wonder if the neighbours would notice the gun shots and come running or perhaps they'd just assume it was a car backfiring, though in all my years I don't think I've ever actually heard a car backfiring, have you?'

'Shut up,' he snarled.

'Okay,' said Joseph simply. 'You've got the gun.'

'I'm not stupid. I'm not a stupid man, Joseph. Do you think I'm a stupid man? Is that it?'

'No.'

'You're coming with me, right now, in my truck and we're getting away from here.'

'No,' said Joseph firmly. 'I'm not.'

'What? I've got a gun, in case you hadn't

noticed,' and he waved it around a little to convince Joseph.

'Which you are not going to use. We both know that. Fire it in here and the cops will have the place surrounded in minutes. SWAT team'll cut you down before you even climb into that fancy pick-up you got parked out front. Even if they don't, how far do you think you'd get with a handful of small bills and an APB out on you?'

'Get up,' demanded Merve, who was in no mood to listen.

'No, and it's for your own good. If I leave here with you, you could be tempted to do something very stupid, like killing me. Think it through, Merve, if you make me leave here with you, what else can you do to shut me up? But people are going to miss me. I told my friend, the retired cop in my building all about Macy and Coach Geller and he wondered out loud how pissed off it must have made you to hear all about it.' Joseph hadn't bothered a convalescing Eddie Filan with his theories but Merve Williams didn't know that. 'And I mentioned my suspicions to one of Lopez's colleagues at Antoinette Irving. What will you do? Try and find out who I spoke to and kill them, too?' Merve was breathing hard and looking around the

269

room like he hoped a hole would suddenly open up somewhere so that he could dive into it. 'I don't think you're the serial-killer type, Merve, do you?' Merve lowered the gun just a little now. It looked like he had begun to realise the magnitude of his problems.

'This neighbourhood's a good one now, there's CCTV cameras all round here,' added Joseph. 'They're all gonna show me driving down the street, parking up and coming in here, then leaving with you. How you going to avoid the gun being seen? Once the police know it was Macy who Geller was seeing they're gonna put you right at the top of their list of suspects.'

'Shut up! Shut up!' screamed Merve. 'Just shut up!' And this time he didn't care that his neighbours might hear. Merve was beyond caring. Joseph could tell that by the way he had switched the gun around. He was no longer pointing it at Joseph. Instead he pressed the barrel hard against his own head. Then he closed his eyes.

19

'It doesn't have to end like this, Merve,' reasoned Joseph, but Merve wasn't listening. Instead, he cocked the gun and pressed the barrel so firmly against the side of his own skull that Joseph was worried it might go off by accident. 'Look at me, Merve, look at me,' urged Joseph, and the hardware-store owner finally opened his dead eyes then looked over at Joseph like he had forgotten he was still in the room. 'Sure you've got some big explaining to do but you had your reasons for going down there that night to confront Macy's teacher. Maybe you didn't mean to kill Hernando Lopez but if we don't hear your side of the story it will die with you and everyone will say that Merve Williams was just a cold-blooded murderer. Think about your wife and children, Merve, everything you've done for them, all your hard work in the store, it'll all be for nothing. Do you really want Macy to go through life knowing her father killed himself because of what she did

271

with some dumb, old married guy? Imagine how that's gonna make her feel. Think about your other little girl. You want Laura to grow up knowing everybody thinks her daddy was a killer without you explaining yourself. That kind of thing can send a girl right off the rails. Just imagine how it could affect her. Both those girls are going to need their daddy, Merve, you know that.'

Joseph was not a gambling man but he figured there was about a fifty-fifty chance of Merve Williams leaving the building lifeless on a gurney. Merve looked like he didn't care if he lived or died. Then his expression changed. His eyes lifted and he looked towards the door like he was pleading to someone. Joseph turned to find Macy Williams standing in the open doorway, huge raindrop tears welling in her eyes.

'Macy, honey.' It took Merve a lot of effort just to get those two words out.

'Daddy?' she asked, shocked by the scene in front of her. 'What are you doing?' She meant the gun, which Merve still held pressed hard against his head but he couldn't answer her and, when she spoke again, Joseph realised she had already heard enough of their conversation to understand it all. 'What have you done?'

Merve Williams let out a long anguished moan then his arm fell down to his side, the gun still hanging limply in his hand.

'Why don't you put the gun down and tell us what happened. Tell Macy here what you did. Did you intend to kill Hernando Lopez that night?'

'It wasn't like that,' Merve told his daughter softly. 'You got to believe me, honey, it wasn't like that.'

Joseph slowly got to his feet and, without making any sudden movements, he walked over to Merve and held out his hand. When Merve didn't respond, Joseph moved it lower and he took hold of the gun by its barrel. At first Merve continued to grip onto it but when Joseph looked him directly in the eye he finally released his grip and let go. Joseph took the gun, ejected the magazine and put it in his jacket pocket then he put the gun in his belt and sat down again.

'Oh my god, I don't believe it,' whispered his daughter.

Macy was a slim, firm-bodied young woman but somehow she still had the face of a child, at least in Joseph's eyes. Coach Geller obviously felt differently.

'It wasn't like that,' said Merve once again. When Joseph spoke, the words were so calm he could have been enquiring about the price of lumber. 'Okay, Merve I believe you,' he said. 'So what *was* it like?'

When Merve finally composed himself long enough to speak, his words weren't intended for Joseph. Instead, his eyes never left Macy's as he tried to reason with his little girl, 'Macy, you got to believe I went down there because of you. I just wanted to reason with this guy, this married guy, tell him to leave my baby alone.'

'I don't want to hear this,' sobbed Macy.

'How'd you find out about Macy and her teacher?'

'You changed,' he said, still addressing his daughter. 'Staying out till all hours, back-chatting your momma, not giving a damn what your daddy said no more, keeping secrets from us. You never used to be like that, not till you started seeing him.'

'So all this is my fault?' she asked him as if he had lost his wits.

'And then I found the keys,' he said flatly.

'Where'd you find them, Daddy?' she raised her voice defiantly.

'In your bag.' He held up his hand. 'I know I shouldn't have looked in there, but if it had been drugs they'd have said I done the right thing. I knew right there and then those keys were for the school, they all had the initials A.I.H.S. stamped on them and the numbers of the classrooms.'

'So you took the keys and went down there instead of Macy,' said Joseph, 'so how'd you ensure that Macy wouldn't see the keys were gone or head down there.'

'He drove me over to my gran's. Said I didn't spend nearly enough time with family, and it was about time I started. He drove me all the way to Newark. There's no way I could get back in time, and my mobile and the keys – were back in my bag at the apartment. He said we were just popping out for five minutes, and I didn't need all that junk,' Macy answered for him, dropping her hands from her mascara-stained face.

Merve nodded. 'Then you waited till evening and went down there.'

Merve nodded again. 'Without her around, I thought it would be easier to make him leave the school, the city...'

'Jesus Christ, Daddy, you are such a fool.'

'Don't talk to me like that, Macy,' her father warned her, as if the last vestiges of his authority were melting away in front of his eyes.

'But it didn't work out like that did it?'

'No.'

'Did you even know who you were expecting to see there?'

Merve shook his head.

'But you found Lopez walking alone along the school's darkened corridors. A young, handsome, charismatic teacher with – how did you put it? – "a way with the young ones", and you naturally assumed...'

Merve's silence was admission enough. 'Oh, Daddy, no!' cried Macy and she slumped onto the floor and started sobbing on her knees right there on the carpet in front of them both. 'What have you done?'

'And you attacked him?' prompted Joseph.

'I ... I can't remember. I said some things... I was angry and I went towards him... I was angry and... She's only seventeen... You're a father Joseph... You understand.'

'Sure,' he said but he did not.

'He pulled a knife,' said Merve hopefully, perhaps he was imagining a courtroom and some future plea of self defence.

'Of course he did, Merve, he was being attacked. He feared for his life. You said you were going to kill him for messing with your daughter. Lopez probably thought you were deranged. So he made his big mistake, he pulled out the knife he'd taken from

Jermaine Letts and he waved it at you, told you to get back. That must have enraged you. What kind of a teacher sleeps with his students and carries a knife? And he's telling you to go back. But you didn't go back, did you, Merve?'

'He jabbed the knife at me, not once but a bunch of times. I remember getting so angry at this punk standing there waving his knife around. I stepped forwards, he cut my hand.' He held up his hand to show Joseph a red mark on the palm, like it was a reason to kill someone. 'But I managed to grab the knife and then... I don't remember.'

'Yes, you do.'

'No.' He was shaking his head again. 'We were close together, struggling, it was desperate and somehow the knife...'

'Ended up sticking out of his chest?'

'Yes.'

Macy Williams was lying on the floor now, her face obscured by her long, blonde hair, her sobbing deep and breathless but regular as a heartbeat.

'Then he fell against the wall,' continued Joseph, 'leaving blood there and more on the wooden floor, before he staggered into his classroom. He went to the far window, probably thought he could call for help but no one heard him and that's how he left that big smear of blood against the glass.' The one Joseph had seen as he emerged from his cab the next morning. 'And what did you do, Merve? When you saw this guy dying in front of you?'

'I panicked.'

'You panicked.'

'Yes, I remembered I still had the keys in my pocket so I found the one that matched the number on his door and...'

'You locked him in there.'

'Yes,' Merve cried, covering his face, 'It wasn't supposed to go like that. I panicked. I couldn't risk anyone finding out. I had to do it. Don't you see? Had to.'

'Then what?'

'I ran.'

'But you still had the keys?'

'I threw them in the bushes outside.'

Turning to Macy, Joseph demanded, 'Didn't you ever wonder where the keys were?'

Shrugging, Macy wiped a clot of snot from her nose with the cuff of her jacket. 'Figured one of my brothers hid them. I gave them hell over that. Then I just figured they'd show up some time.'

'Meanwhile, Lopez was bleeding to death.

He realised nobody could hear him from the window so he turned back to the door to find you'd locked him in. He needed help and he needed it fast. He was probably banking on reaching the principal's office to phone for an ambulance. Instead he got as far as taking the keys he borrowed and putting them in the lock but he'd lost a lot of blood by then. He must have passed out then and died right there on the floor of his own classroom.

Hearing all of this while his daughter sobbed in front of him seemed to exhaust Merve. He kept repeating 'I'm sorry, so sorry' over and over again between the tears.

'Sorry ain't gonna bring poor Lopez back?' said Joseph. 'Tell me, Merve, how long was it before you realised you'd killed the wrong man?'

'Macy came back the night they arrested Geller, told me she loved him, said she was going to run off with him when the cops realised they'd got the wrong man and there was nothing I could do about it. It was just what I was trying to stop by going down there and it turned out she's going anyway.'

'Careful, Macy,' said Joseph and she stopped sobbing long enough to look up into his eyes. 'He might not be such a great catch when the school board fire him for sleeping with his pupils.'

'Fuck you,' she screamed and he could easily see how she could be a member of Rihanna Letts' gang.

'I think I've heard enough,' announced Joseph and he got up to leave.

'Where you going?' asked Merve.

'Home.'

'You can't tell anyone, Joseph,' pleaded Merve. 'For my wife, my family, you can't tell anyone, you hear?'

'He won't have to, Daddy.'

Both men turned to see Macy staggering to her feet, and moving towards the phone on the desk.

'You can't control me anymore. Family? Hah!' Meanwhile, Joseph saw her pressing down on three digits.

'Hello, officer,' she spoke into the mouthpiece, her voice shaky. 'I need to report a crime...'

Joseph left the building, pushing the door out against a harsh wind. It was going to be a long, cold winter in the Bronx. Outside, Assistant Chief McCavity was supervising Merve's transfer into the squad car.

Merve's hands were cuffed behind his

back and there was no sign of Macy. It looked like she wasn't going to be following Daddy down to the precinct any time soon. Merve looked all in. By now, he was probably even relieved to have been arrested. After all, he knew he had killed an innocent man and he would have to live with that for the rest of his life.

As Joseph was walking away, McCavity called after him and followed him over to his cab. 'What if he had just calmly shot you and run?' she asked. 'You think of that?'

'Yeah. But Merve is a family man,' he said. 'He's nothing without his wife and kids, it's all he ever talks about. He ain't the running kind.'

'I still can't believe this was just about a schoolgirl having a fling with her teacher,' she said.

'Money and fucking,' said Joseph softly to himself.

'What?' asked McCavity.

'Nothing.'

'I'm getting a little pissed at you, Mr Solinka, you wanna know why?'

'You don't have to be a detective to work it out,' he answered dryly.

'It's probably not what you think,' she said calmly, 'my guess is you reckon I see you as an irritant, someone who gets in my way and makes me look bad when I don't come up with the right answer, when you have such an uncanny knack of just stumbling across the solution all on your lonesome.'

That was exactly what he thought. 'Not at all,' he said.

'No, my beef with you is that you're not on our side. Instead, you're off doing your own thing, instead of sharing your great insights with us early on and letting us get on with the investigating,' Joseph opened his mouth to say something, but she held up a hand. 'Let me finish. I heard an interesting thing about you. I asked one of my guys to find out a little more about the man who goes around solving crimes in his neighbourhood, and you know what he came back with?'

Joseph shook his head.

'It seems you've applied to join us,' she laughed. 'Twice, apparently, turned down each time because of your inability to provide a reference.'

Joseph was becoming angry now. It looked as if McCavity was only telling him this so that she could mock his background and ridicule his ambitions. He hoped it made her feel better to belittle him like this, here in the street. McCavity continued, 'Well, I've seen enough to know that you are far from corrupt or you'd have taken that drug dealer's money when he offered it instead of helping to bring him down like you did. I also know you've got a mind like a whip, 'cos you figured out who killed Hernando Lopez before any of my officers and, despite what you might think of them, they are some smart guys I've got working for me, believe me. I like to have clever people in my team, Joseph.' It was the first time she had used his Christian name. 'How'd you like to work for me?'

'Me?' he asked dumbly. 'But my refer-ences...' It was all he could think to offer by way of an answer.

'Mmm, yes, well, what better reference than the testimony of an Assistant Chief in the NYPD. I think that ought to cut through some of the HR-generated, red-tape bull-shit, don't you? Then I guess we'll really see what you're made of. I can tell you're a little shocked, so I'm going to give you time to think about it. You've got one day.' And she handed him a business card. 'Call me when you've made up your mind.'

She pressed the card into his outstretched palm. 'But don't leave it too late, I'm quite a busy police officer, in case you hadn't noticed.'

She started to walk away.

'But...' he said. 'I don't...'

'Understand?' she asked. 'I'm not an idiot, Joseph. I have good detectives working for me for a reason. They solve cases and that does me not a little good in the process. In return, I make sure they're looked after. I like my boys to do well. Besides, there's another reason. I'm an advocate of the Lyndon Johnson school of thinking.'

'Which is?'

'I'd rather have you in my tent pissing out than outside my tent pissing in,' she told him firmly. 'That's why your application to join the NYPD just jumped to the top of the pile. Have a nice day now.'

And she left him staring down at the business card in his hand like he was clutching a winning ticket in the lottery.

20

The Crips' Killers went pretty meekly in the end. Of course it helped that they were caught red-handed right in the middle of unloading another batch of plasma TVs from the back of their pick-up. Rihanna Letts cursed and threatened the uniformed officers of the 41st Precinct. She also spat at them, kicked out and tried to throw punches, but they had all been selected for their size and were able to literally lift the screaming girl off her feet and march her and her fellow gang members right into the waiting squad cars. It was about as open and shut a case as any Joseph had seen and he had witnessed this one from a balcony in the project, which neatly overlooked the spot previously classed as the turf of the Crips' Killers.

McCavity had been as good as her word when he called her that morning. He'd agreed to come and work for her but asked for one small favour.

'Jesus Christ,' she said, 'you ain't even

joined yet and you're asking for favours.'

'I know,' he said, 'and it's not even really your area but I was hoping you might speak to someone.' Then he had told her all about Eddie Filan, the ex-cop who'd been brutally beaten by a gang, and she'd agreed to make a call.

'I guess I owe you for the Merve Williams thing,' she conceded.

A film crew from an evening news channel had somehow gained word of the impending raid in advance and trailed the arresting officers as they moved in for the kill. There was some juicy footage for that night's bulletins, run above the caption 'Juvenile Girl Gangs of the South Bronx – the shocking unseen truth'. Joseph watched the film clips of Rihanna Letts being lifted off her feet like a toddler having a tantrum. Her face was distorted on the TV, pixilated, to prevent her identity becoming known by the viewing public, after all, as yet, she had never been convicted of any crime. Cloaking her identity was a strange precaution because only someone who had no idea who Rihanna Letts was would find the footage anonymous. Anyone who knew the girl at all would instantly recognise the shrill, screaming mouth, its expletives bleeped out for the viewing public, leaving few words that could be aired safely. They would then identify the burly-framed female as the eldest Letts girl.

'Your momma must be awful proud,' said Joseph to himself as the footage was concluded.

Rihanna Letts was looking at jail time, pure and simple and, after what her crew had done to Eddie, Joseph felt little sympathy.

A few days later, Joseph's cell phone trilled insistently at him from his inside pocket. 'Damn it,' he said, as he tried to open his apartment door without dropping the groceries from the three brown paper bags his arms were wrapped around. He twisted the key in the lock and turned so he could knock the door open with his rear then he hastily dropped the groceries on the Formica counter top and delved inside his jacket to retrieve the phone.

'Yeah,' he said breathlessly for it had been a long, hard climb up the stairs with the groceries in his arms.

'Joseph it's me,' she said, before adding, 'Brigitte,' as if he might have forgotten the sound of her voice in the time since they had last spoken.

'Brigitte,' he answered brightly. 'Hi, how are you doing?' Why did it suddenly seem so uncomfortable to talk with this woman he had always felt so natural with?

'I was just calling because I assumed you'd be worried about Ardo.'

'Ardo?' he asked unsurely. 'Why? What's happened to him?'

'Well,' she said a little impatiently. 'I thought you'd want to know if the school was going to take any action against him.'

'Action against...' he began, not comprehending. 'Sorry, I'm not sure I understand. What has Ardo done that would require any action to be taken against him?'

'Technically, he allowed a set of very important keys away from his person.' It took him a moment to realise she was talking about the time Geller got hold of Ardo's keys and not the day when the janitor let Joseph borrow them. 'That led to an abuse. In this case, it resulted in the death of a teacher.' She made poor Ardo sound like an accomplice. 'But Principal Decker felt that it could just as easily have allowed the wrong kind of person into the school building while the children were still there.' And since when did you ever agree with anything Principal Decker said, wondered Joseph, hardly recognising the woman he was speaking to now. Clearly Ardo was being accused of assisting paedophiles as well as murderers, poor guy.

'However,' she continued, 'in the end it was agreed there was a safety issue, because Ardo was expected to wear his keys on his belt at all times and he couldn't very well do that while he was washing the school windows from a ladder, in case he fell.'

What she meant was Decker had ordered Ardo to wear his keys on his belt at all times but that was a dumb and unsafe thing to do, so Ardo had ignored him and lost his keys as a result. Decker might have wanted to use the incident to get rid of Ardo but, like every sensible, spineless public servant in the state, he will have taken legal advice first. Any lawyer worth a cent would have advised Decker that Ardo would have a strong case against Antoinette Irving High and its principal if he was fired for taking his keys off his belt before climbing a ladder.

'The school are getting the locks changed and having new keys cut. They are going to ensure there is somewhere secure for Ardo to leave his keys when he washes the windows in future.'

'So he's off the hook?' asked Joseph a little impatiently.

'I guess you could say so. That wasn't the only reason I called by the way,' she cleared her throat. 'I wanted to thank you for teaching me to shoot. Maybe I shouldn't be, but I feel a lot safer walking the streets now thanks to you.'

'That's okay. I was going to call you, too, really I was. I wanted to say sorry I shot away the other night without coming in for coffee. I hope you don't think I was rude.'

'It's no biggy,' she said, somewhat self-consciously. There was a pause then, a momentary lull in conversation where each of them was waiting for the other to say something. Finally she filled the void of silence. 'I've really got to go, Joseph,' she said a little coldly. 'I've got a date tonight.'

'Oh,' he said, not knowing why he should be so surprised.

'I mean, it's a kind of date,' she began. 'No, well, I mean it *is* a date, actually.' She seemed mightily unsure about it, though, thought Joseph. 'Just this guy I met through a friend. She's a teacher at Antoinette Irving as well and he's, well, like I say, her friend. He seems like a nice guy.'

And why are you telling me all this, thought Joseph, as if I didn't know. Still, he couldn't help but feel a pang of something, knowing that Brigitte would be spending the evening with another man, though it sounded more like a blind date than a full-blown romance.

'Anyway, its not as if you and I...' she continued.

'No, exactly.'

'Well then,' she concluded.

'I probably shouldn't keep you then,' he said. 'And I promised I would bring Eddie his groceries.'

There didn't seem to be anything left to add and Joseph was about to say goodbye to Brigitte De Moyne when she suddenly said, 'I was thinking...'

'What?'

'You never did tell me who you wanted to be when you were a little boy.'

'Does it matter now?'

'I'm curious, that's all.' Her tone was light again, almost playful. 'I'd just like to know who the ace detective wanted to be before he grew up.'

'Well, I'd have thought it was obvious.'

'No,' she said. 'Not really.'

'Where I lived in Lagos we used to get all the British and American TV and films.'

'And?'

'I was a young boy in a big city, dreaming

of adventures in far-off places.'

'Yeah, so?'

'Obviously I wanted to be James Bond.'

Brigitte laughed. 'Oh my, that's hilarious.' And she tried unsuccessfully to stifle her giggles.

'What's so funny about that?'

'Well, for starters, James Bond is English or Scottish or something and, well...'

'What?'

She said solemnly, with mock seriousness, 'I hate to be the one to break your heart here, Joseph, but you don't look Scottish.'

'Really,' he said it like he was devastated. 'Damn.'

She was laughing freely now and it seemed to take all of the harshness and resentment out of her voice, cutting through the tension between them. 'I think I know why you wanted to be James Bond,' she said.

'You do, do you?'

'Yeah,' she pronounced confidently. 'Because he always gets the girl at the end.'

'Maybe that's it.'

When Brigitte rang off, Joseph was left with the undeniable conclusion that it was possible to be friends with a woman but it was a whole lot harder to stay friends with her if she wanted more. The sad fact was

Joseph had no free time in his life and no space in his heart for anything else right now. There were too many people depending on him.

It would take more than the small matter of a fractured patella to keep Eddie Filan out of the Mucky Duck for ever. The Black Swan was an Irish-American bar that served the right brand of whisky with the absolute minimum of intrusive conversation from the barman. There was no piped music, no overhead TV-broadcasting highlights of last night's ball game and no pseudo-Irish paraphernalia decorating the place. As Eddie put it, 'They don't got no bicycles, no Davy lamps or any little, green leprechauns hanging from the ceiling and that's just fine with me'. The bar was a short drive out of the project in Joseph's cab, which would have been a lot easier than Eddie's insisted method of travel, hobbling there on a pair of crutches in a protracted stop-start journey that was punctuated with colourful curse words along the way.

'You've always got to insist on doing it the hard way, don't you?' asked Joseph

'What's a matter wit' you now?' asked Eddie grumpily, as he hauled his frame along, 'a couple of days ago you were bugging me to get out of my apartment. The minute I do that, you're bugging me again! I can't win with you, Joseph, you know that?'

He supposed Eddie had a point. Joseph had been worried about the old guy. He had seemed to lose his appetite; for food, for company, for life, after the beating he had taken. The physical injuries were one thing, but it was the psychological damage the once-hard man had received that concerned Joseph the most. Eddie's confidence had been all but destroyed in that attack. Joseph was willing to bet he had no idea how to cope with a beating received from a bunch of girls. Even if he had been physically capable of it, he doubted whether Eddie would have been able to force himself to fight back.

Since then, all efforts to get him out of his apartment had failed. Then word had gone round that the police had rolled up the notorious Crips' Killers and the mood of everyone on the project had lifted. Suddenly, the residents of Highbridge became more visible. It was like the whole apartment block had breathed a collective sigh of relief. The very next day Eddie had suggested an excursion to the Mucky Duck and

Joseph had been delighted, readily offering to drive him down there.

'I go on my own two legs or I don't go at all,' the old curmudgeon had snarled and that had been the end of the debate.

Now he propelled himself along in the stiff-legged way of the invalid. 'Yomi forgiven you for getting his girlfriend's pop arrested?'

'Hasn't said much about it. I don't think he's seeing Laura any more.'

'Mmm, that ain't no surprise but he understands, does he?'

'I think so.'

'What about her father? Got to be looking at a lot of jail time.'

'They're still evaluating him, psych tests and profiling and whatever the mind doctors do. It might surprise you to learn this but I'm hearing they might let him out on bail. Even McCavity is talking about just charging him with manslaughter without criminal malice and she's no longer pushing for Murder One. I think the DA told her that Merve was probably deranged and there aren't too many votes in those type of cases.'

'Jesus, after what he did to that teacher?'

'I know, but they're saying his mind was disturbed on account of his sweet, innocent daughter being corrupted by her teacher like that.'

'You gotta be kidding me!'

'I'm not saying I agree with it. I'm saying they think that's how he saw it. It's what made him snap.'

'Jesus, he didn't even stab the right guy.'

For the umpteenth time, Eddie had stopped in the street, straightened himself and taken in a few slow, deep breaths. At this rate, he would be exhausted before he got there. Joseph secretly hoped he could get the man full enough of beer and Irish whisky that they could both hop a cab back afterwards. The irony of paying someone else to drive him home after a few drinks was not lost on Joseph.

The journey was clearly taking more out of Eddie than he'd hoped. Joseph stood placidly to one side, emotionless. 'What you looking at?' asked Eddie. 'You got some place to be? Then go.'

'Someone's got to watch your ass, make sure you don't fall flat on it.'

Eddie mumbled something inaudible and they set off again. 'I hear the cops raided the lockups, picked up a gang of young fucks for holding some stolen shit there,' observed Eddie self-consciously.

'I heard that, too,' said Joseph.

'You sure you didn't know anything about that bust?' asked Eddie.

'Me? How could I?' He hadn't told Eddie about McCavity yet or the fact he would soon be working for her.

Eddie thought for a moment. 'Mmm, well, don't s'pose they busted the whole gang but at least they got what was coming to 'em.'

He could tell Eddie was searching for any sign that Joseph knew he had taken a beating from a gang of girls. Joseph could see no point to admitting that. As it stood, he knew the old man was past his prime and he'd been jumped by some pretty-frightening individuals. It made little difference to Joseph that they happened to be born female. Either way, nobody would be seeing them round here for a while.

Joseph decided to change the subject and Eddie seemed glad of it.

'The doctor told me you were lucky. He said you had a hard head.'

'Oh yeah?' answered Eddie. 'What did you say?'

'I told him he didn't know the half of it. I said you had the thickest head in Jersey. I told him 'this is the man who took on Big Joey Moretti and beat him in a fair fight, kind of.'

Eddie chuckled. 'And what did he say to that? He even heard of Joey Moretti?'

'Nope.'

'Sweet Jesus,' said Eddie wryly. 'It's a man's curse to outlive the usefulness of his deeds.'

'That is very profound, Eddie, who said that?'

'I did,' answered Eddie indignantly. 'Just now.'

'Oh.'

'Oh what? You saying you didn't think I was smart enough to come out with something profound. Is that what you are saying?'

'No,' answered Joseph, then he said, 'Actually yes, normally you can't utter a sentence without it containing motherfuckin' this and cocksuckin' that.'

'You serious?'

'Completely, everything is always "fuck yous" and "get the fuck out" or "the dumbass motherfucks don't do this" or "them cocksuckin', dirt-bag low-lifes should do that". And this is only when we're watching the evening news together. I hate to think what you say when you're with your drinking buddies from the old precinct.'

Eddie laughed. 'I guess you got a point

there. Since my poor gal died, I've had no one to slap me down for my cussing. I was a cop for forty years, Joseph, I seen some things that make a few cuss words seem...'

'Unimportant?'

'Yeah,' he nodded. 'But it's bad. My mother, god rest her, she used to say it's the sign of a limited vocabulary. It ain't a good thing to be always cussing like I do.' He thought for a moment. 'You know what? I'm gonna stop, right here, today. I am, truly.'

'You really mean that?'

'Course not, you sorry-ass, dumb-shit, cocksuckin' motherfucker. Now, get a move on or we ain't ever gonna get there,' and he set his crutches in motion again, 'oh and you don't have to go worrying about my drinking buddies, neither.'

'No?'

'All gone, dead or retired to Florida, which is the same fucking thing if you ask me.'

'None left, huh?'

'You the only one, Joseph, the only one who'll still drink with a twisted old fuck like me. Why do you do it? Tell me, why do you bother with me?'

'You want to hear the truth?'

'Give it to me straight, doc.'

'I get a cheque each month from the welfare.' Eddie was laughing now. 'They said, "someone has to do it, Joseph, someone has to stop him from writing to us and calling us up all the time to complain. Take the miserable S.O.B. to a bar and we'll pay you. We'll even give you a green card". There, that's the truth, Eddie. I'm sorry you had to hear it from me like that.'

They were both laughing now.

'So that's it then. The only reason you spend time with me, you miserable fuck?'

'Yep,' said Joseph. 'Like you Americans are fond of saying "that's all she wrote".'

Eddie laughed again. 'Yeah, well, we got a way with words in this country but then so have you. I like the way you Nigerians say stuff. Now that is some truly profound shit. You got any more of those sayings? They cheer me up.'

'Okay.' He thought for a while.

'Come on, then,' urged Eddie.

'Wait a moment, I'm thinking. Okay, I got one. It means the same as your "there's more than one way to skin a cat".'

'I'm all ears.'

Joseph put on the deep, exaggerated, Africanised voice of a man who has never once left his neighbourhood in Lagos. 'When a man steals your wife, there's no better revenge than to let him keep her.'

'Oh, that's a good one,' laughed the old man. 'I'll buy you a drink for that.'

'If we ever get there.'

'Shut the fuck up.'

They rounded a corner and the cheerless, green sign of the Black Swan came into view. Joseph realised he really wanted a drink. It had been a tough week for everybody, but he knew there were people all around him with bigger problems. Eddie for one. He was growing old and had to face the fact that he was no longer the man he used to be. Yomi had been forced to hear the testimony of the heartbroken mother of a murdered boy, just so he could finally learn that it wasn't cool to carry a knife, then he'd lost his first girlfriend because his father couldn't resist playing the policeman. Coach Geller had discovered the tragic consequences of a mid-life tryst with a teenage girl, while Merve Williams was forced to live the rest of his life knowing he stabbed an innocent man to death because of it. As Eddie was fond of saying, it was a crazy, mixed-up, fucked-up world out there. It seemed to Joseph now, as he looked back on the events of that fateful night at Antoinette Irving, that a whole lot of people had been forced to learn some tough lessons.

The publishers hope that this book has given you enjoyable reading. Large Print Books are especially designed to be as easy to see and hold as possible. If you wish a complete list of our books please ask at your local library or write directly to:

Dales Large Print Books
Magna House, Long Preston,
Skipton, North Yorkshire.
BD23 4ND

This Large Print Book, for people
who cannot read normal print,
is published under the auspices of

THE ULVERSCROFT FOUNDATION

... we hope you have enjoyed this book.
Please think for a moment about those
who have worse eyesight than you ...
and are unable to even read or enjoy
Large Print without great difficulty.

You can help them by sending a
donation, large or small, to:

**The Ulverscroft Foundation,
1, The Green, Bradgate Road,
Anstey, Leicestershire, LE7 7FU,
England.**
or request a copy of our brochure for
more details.

The Foundation will use all donations
to assist those people who are visually
impaired and need special attention
with medical research, diagnosis
and treatment.

Thank you very much for your help.